LOVE IS SOUR

MAYBE IT'S LUST?

NICKI GRACE

NICKI GRACE NOVELS

To anyone who has experienced the roller coaster of love I hope you found your happiness and if not, I'm sure it's on the way.

CHAPTER 1

The tears would not stop coming, and the pain in her heart was agonizing. It delivered a rushing blow so vehement that Piper wondered how she would ever survive this.

How did this happen? Why did this happen? Is this what I deserved for trusting a man at his word?

That evening, the questions "How?" and "Why?" made their rounds in her head for the millionth time. As common sense set in, the simple truth that he was involved with someone else was clear.

Why wouldn't he be?

They talked a lot, mainly through text, which should have been a red flag, and she barely saw him.

But she loved him. That's where all of this went wrong. Her heart wanted him; he'd made her feel loved, adored, and desired. The long-distance didn't matter to her; only him, and if she were being honest, she still loved him.

Was everything he said really all a lie?

"Stop it," Lish said from across the room.

She was sitting at Piper's kitchen table, putting together a list of different ways they could kill Scott. She told Piper it was just for fun, but Piper wasn't sure Lish didn't have other plans.

"You've started crying again. And that means you are thinking. Stop it. He doesn't deserve your tears."

"You are right. He doesn't. He deserves my foot up his ass. It doesn't even have to be my foot; it can be someone else's just as long as it hurts," she grunted, crossing her arms.

"I like that," Lish said, holding up her pen. "I'll add that one to the list."

Piper sniffed and grabbed another tissue.

"I should have listened to you, but I felt such a connection to him. I'm so stupid."

Lish dropped the pen and joined her best friend on the couch, pulling her in for a hug.

"Aww, come here. Getting your heart broken is not your fault, and it does not make you stupid. What you do with this information will determine that."

"What do you mean?" Piper asked, straightening.

"Can he talk his way back into your life?"

"Absolutely not!"

"You say that now, but love is a tricky thing. You are going to want to forgive him. I'm not saying that to call you weak. I've just been there. Do you remember Justin?"

Piper nodded. Justin was an abusive boyfriend that Lish had dated off and on for five years. Their relationship made Piper and Quentin look like a walk in the park. He was no good for Lish, but that didn't stop his presence in her life.

At one point, Lish was so lost, she said living a life with his rage, jealousy and neurosis were better than living apart from him. It wasn't until Justin slapped Lish's younger sister, Jamie, 15 at the time, that she saw how low she'd sunk. The nonexistent value of her own self-worth manifested itself so distinctly, she could almost touch it. She broke it off shortly thereafter and never looked back.

"I'm so angry right now. I don't see myself accepting him back, Lish."

"Has he called?"

"No, but I called him."

"And?"

"There was no answer. He will likely call me tomorrow. Sometimes he skips days."

Hearing herself explain his schedule of picking and choosing when he communicated with her caused her to place her face in her hands and scream.

"I'M SO STUPID!"

"Didn't I say stop it? Let's talk about something else. How is Aunt Delores? Is that a new color on your toes? I heard Vince and Lacy at it again earlier when you were showering. Something about, lick me like a cat."

"You sure it wasn't 'lick my cat'?" Piper said, trying desperately to allow her mind to escape into the sicko world of Vince and Lacy.

"They have a cat?" Lish asked,.

"No. I was assuming Lacy said it to Vince."

"Nope, Vince said it."

"Yuck. Next subject, please. I don't want to imagine what the hell he meant."

Piper sighs and shakes her head. Then, answering the questions in the order Lish had asked them, Piper said, "My Aunt is trying to crochet blankets to keep her mind busy, which hasn't worked out so well due to the pain. And no, this is not new polish. I simply mixed two colors I already owned."

"Hmm, I know! Didn't you tell me you got a callback for an interview?"

3

Piper wiped her face with a fresh tissue and smiled a little.

"I did say that. It's for a hospital called Juniper Creek Medical."

"I've seen that place. It's nice. Getting a job there would be like living in one of those medical TV shows you love."

"It would."

Piper felt her spirits lift, then abruptly drop again.

"But I'm not likely to get it. My interview isn't for two weeks, on the 12th, because they have so many candidates."

"You can't think that way. Besides, look at the bright side. It gives you more time to prepare for those 'where do you see yourself in five years?' type of questions.

"That is true," Piper agreed. "And I could use the practice since I haven't been on an interview in a while."

"Luckily for you. I have a great idea."

"What?"

"First, we will do interview practice questions. When we're done, I'll take you to dinner at your favorite restaurant downtown as a congratulations from me to you on getting the interview."

Lish smiled proudly, and Piper opened her mouth.

"And I will not accept no for an answer."

Closing her mouth, Piper sat back and said, "You always have the best ideas."

Scott sent Piper a good morning text the following day, but she didn't answer. She was hoping it would prompt him to call her right away, but it didn't. His predictable routine suggested he wouldn't call her until the end of her workday.

Fine by her. Yelling at work wasn't professional anyway.

Keeping her mind on the positive—an upcoming job interview with a fantastic company—gave her the energy to get things done, and the first half of Piper's morning flew by. She submitted claims, cleaned up her desk, and even took care of the cages before her usual time.

As it neared the lunch hour, Piper's phone lit up on her desk. The caller ID displayed 'unknown', and Piper's heart rate increased. Snatching up the phone, she hurried outside.

"Hello?"

Silence.

After removing the phone from her ear to glance at the screen, she was sure the caller was still there.

Taking a stab in the dark, Piper asked, "Is this about Scott?"

"I guess you aren't so stupid after all," a woman said on the other end.

The girl sounded young, a lot younger than Piper. She had a slight accent, which wasn't easily pegged, and her discourteous approach caused Piper instant agitation.

Piper suddenly felt attacked by mixed emotions. Should she end the call with the juvenile bitch now? Or, stick around and possibly get some answers?

Deciding on the latter, Piper said the first thing that came to mind to get the woman talking.

"Is this his wife?"

"His wife is dead," the woman scoffed. "But he does have plans to marry me. So, you may as well leave him alone."

The comment made Piper cringe.

He had plans to marry this woman? Never mind all that, she reminded herself, *just keep her talking.*

"I saw you with him. No need to threaten me about dumping his sorry ass. I'm better than that."

The woman laughed.

"Are you trying to imply that I'm not? You have no idea

what he and I have. You can only hope to have a man love you as much as Scott loves me, but until then, go and find your own because you can't have mine."

Piper surprised herself when she said. "He is playing you, and you still want him? What is wrong with you?"

"Don't worry about me, worry about yourself, and stay the fuck away from him or you will be sorry," the woman ended the call.

Piper stood there holding the phone to her ear, letting the threats of some confused stranger penetrate deeper than they should have. This woman had called to harass her over a man that had lied to them both. Piper was heated and couldn't wait for work to be over because playboy Scott had some explaining to do.

Piper made it home quicker than usual that day. She was driving at least 15 miles per hour over the speed limit and was beyond grateful when she made it home without getting pulled over.

Heading upstairs to her apartment, she saw the girl she and Lish called Legs knocking on Desmond's door. They nodded a cordial hello to one another as Piper passed, and a streak of jealousy reared its ugly head.

They made a cute couple, and the girl probably had the love life with Desmond that Piper only wished she had with Scott.

She found herself wondering what type of man Desmond was. One thing was apparent. He liked tall women. The girl had to be at least 5'10, and Piper was only 5'4.

That all made sense because he was easily over 6'3 himself, but aside from the type of woman he was attracted to, what kind of guy was he? Did he cheat on his girlfriends too? Was he just as manipulative and heartless as Scott?

Piper dropped her mail, purse, and keys on the counter and once again fought to keep her anger at bay. At a time like this, a little shopping would have been an excellent outlet, but hobbies like those were suspended until her account could retain numbers above the double digits.

She said a quick prayer for the position at Juniper. Living with constant monetary restrictions was too hard, and it made returning to stripping a compelling option.

"I will not return to stripping," she promised herself aloud.

Her cell rang, and she pulled it from her purse so quickly it slipped from her hands.

"Hi, Baby," he said, all cheerful and sweet.

"Don't hi Baby me! I know exactly what you have been up to."

Scott had the nerve to sound genuinely confused.

"What are you talking about, Piper?"

"Don't play dumb, Scott. I saw you kissing that woman the other day. I had to go back to NuVive, and there you were with your lips locked on hers."

"Piper, I can explain."

She pulled out a chair and sat down, crossing her arms and squeezing the phone a tad too tight.

"Can you? I'd really love to hear the lie you're about to tell me," she mocked sarcastically.

"I'm not going to lie. It's all truth."

"Okay. First, explain why you weren't at work? Do you make it a habit of starting fights with me, saying you're going back out of town for work, but instead hang out around the city kissing other women?"

"That's not fair. Ryan was sick, so I stayed in town a few more days to make sure he was alright. I didn't call you because I knew you were likely still mad at me, and every-thing was moving so fast. After Ryan got better, I hopped on the first plane and went back to work."

Piper had no comment for that. It sounded like total bullshit to her. Using Ryan as an excuse was too convenient, but she couldn't prove he was lying. Plus, he loved Ryan. Why would he lie about him being sick? Even still, she wasn't ready to simply forgive and put it behind them. Therefore, instead of questioning him further about Ryan, she moved on.

"Explain the woman."

"That was Simone."

"Why in the hell are you kissing Ryan's nanny?"

"It wasn't like that. She kissed me."

"Like that matters. You didn't seem to have any objections at the time."

"I swear to you. You have it all wrong." He took a deep breath. "Admittedly, I should have been upfront about this, but I wasn't."

A small ray of hope leaped forward. She didn't want all she'd believed about him to be a lie.

"Upfront about what?"

"Simone is a young girl with a crush that's gotten out of hand. At first, I thought it would fade. However, now things have escalated, and she has become more aggressive. I need to find a replacement but was trying not to rock the boat because she takes care of Ryan."

"So, you kissed her to keep her calm?" Piper asked in a disbelieving tone.

"No. That has never happened before. I told you her attachment is getting worse. I'm trying to resolve this quickly without causing too much friction."

"If that's true, just fire her, Scott! What you're saying makes no sense."

"If I fire her, who will watch Ryan? I can't up and quit my job. Finding someone to replace her isn't going to be easy because she has pretty much been with him since he was born, and Ryan is attached to her."

"What about his grandparents?"

"They're too old, Piper. Watching him here and there is no problem, but they can't look after him weeks at a time while I work."

Piper didn't know what to say. Even if he was lying, he sounded so sincere and convincing, and most importantly, she had no comeback.

Was it that hard to find a new nanny? And was he only trying to keep the peace at any cost?

"Piper, are you there?"

Her eyes stung as the pain from seeing him and Simone's kiss resurfaced.

"I don't know that I believe you, Scott. Especially since she called me."

"She called you?" Scott said.

"Yes."

"Damn, she must have gone through my phone. I told you she is losing it."

"But if she's losing it, that truly makes her a danger to Ryan."

"You may be right, but my hands are tied. Honestly, though, I don't think she would hurt Ryan."

"Wow, Scott, I didn't know you spoke crazy," Piper snapped.

"Fine. I know nothing for sure, but it's a gut feeling. Bottom line, I have to get her out of my life soon. It's just a very delicate situation, Piper, and I'm doing the best I can. Can you please bear with me?"

The affection and gentleness in his voice towards her pulled at Piper's heartstrings. How in the hell was she supposed to handle this? She was so confused.

"Piper, please believe me. I would never, ever cheat on you," he said. "You are my world, okay?"

"I want to believe you. I do, but—"

9

"Then believe me. You know that I care about you."

Piper wanted to more than anything, but was that wise?

"Where are you right now?" she asked.

"I'm in Milwaukee in this small ass space I rent, wishing I were there with you."

"I'd like to see you. Can you send me a pic?"

"One sec."

After a minute, she heard her text message indicator ding. Sure enough, it was a picture of Scott lying in bed. She tried to ignore how good he looked by focusing on something else. Anything else, but ended up thinking about *someone* else, Desmond.

Dammit, she didn't need to be doing this. Loving one man yet lusting after another.

"Did you get the pic?" he asked.

"I did. You look sexy."

"I'm sure I don't look sexier than you. Why don't you send me one?"

Piper didn't know what her next move should be but falling back into step like nothing ever happened wasn't going to work.

"Scott, I love you. But I need some time."

"But, Baby. I told you the truth. I will figure out a way to get rid of Simone. Give me some time."

"That's exactly what I'm going to do. Give you some time. I'm going to give us both some time. You still kissed her, Scott, and if I hadn't seen you, you weren't going to say anything."

He was silent and then said, "I love you. Don't let what we have end over this."

"I'm not saying I'm going to, but I need space."

"That's fair. Just know that I'm not giving up on us."

Piper ended the call before she became too weak to continue pretending she was so strong.

CHAPTER 2

"Can't I have more time? Do you really have to disconnect my service?"

"Yes, Ms. Fosters," Rita from the cable company said apologetically.

"You haven't made a payment in two months, and the system won't allow for any more extensions. If payment is not received by Monday, services will be suspended."

Had she really not paid her bill in two months? Money was tight, but Piper hadn't realized bills were skipped. At least the interview with Juniper was next week. If she got the job, the debt could be paid. Surely, they could hold it a little longer?

"If I could get one more extension, I should definitely be able to pay it."

"My hands are tied, Ms. Fosters. I'm sorry."

Piper didn't think the woman was sorry at all. Rita from the cable company likely had free cable and Wi-Fi.

Goodbye, fun medical dramas, Piper thought. *It was fun while it lasted.*

"Alright, I'll try to get the money together."

"I hope you do. Have a good day."

"Yeah, yeah," Piper said and ended the call.

It wasn't Rita's fault, and she knew that but blaming her gave Piper a target for her annoyance.

Swinging around to face her computer, only two hours into the workday, it was evident that the whole day would be shitty. For the last few days, there had been no Scott, and soon, there would be no TV shows to escape into either.

Scott had called and sent a few texts, but for the most part, she didn't answer. Being emotionally torn was draining and disconcerting, but hearing his sweet nothings wouldn't give her an unbiased approach on what to do next.

Already he was on her mind constantly, making all her attempts to stay away seem so futile. No matter what she did, thoughts of him would eventually seep in. Particularly in bed at night or when she was showering. It was easy to close her eyes and envision his hands between her legs instead of her own.

After the first day of ignoring his texts, she gave in and responded to an "I love you" message.

Even now, without her consent, her fingers were itching to betray her. Wanting to reach out and ask about his day, agree that they could get through anything and that she didn't want to imagine a life without him.

It was now day three of her limiting their conversations, and since last night, he hadn't said much. The fact both relieved and saddened her. He was due back in town next week for his work break, and she wanted to see him.

Piper repositioned herself in her chair. It was time to stop thinking about Scott. At the moment, he was on the don't stress over list right along with her cable. Her attention was better spent considering the things she could have or may have.

She may have a job with Juniper. Her interview was next

week, and she felt so ready. Lish had thrown out questions while Piper practiced and perfected the answers.

Another good thing was that she could have a few more days with her shows before they shut it off. As a matter of fact, tonight, she was watching scary movies with Jake.

Usually, the night she watched him, the meal was hamburgers 90% of the time, but with all this change occurring in her life, tonight Piper would try her hand at actually cooking a meal. Her food experiment of choice was Lasagna.

There were cooking gadgets collecting dust under her cabinets; time to put those to good use. Piper was never big on cooking, and she still didn't know if she liked it, but she had to get out of this habit of eating so poorly.

A conversation with her aunt last week was another reminder to take better care of herself, live a good life and be happy. Currently, none of those things were effectively taking place.

She stuffed a letter into an envelope that welcomed a new client and their pet to the clinic, sealed it, and dropped it in the pile of items that needed stamps.

Her phone lit up. She assumed it was Scott and quickly picked it up. It wasn't Scott. It was her cousin Chloe getting back to her.

Chloe: Sorry, it took forever. I just saw your text. Yes, I got my clothes, and they are so cute. I wore it last weekend when Reggie and I went to a Caribbean festival downtown.

Piper: Fun! Do you have any pics?

Chloe: Yeah, one sec.

It didn't take long for an image of Chloe hugging her husband, Reginald, to come in. Piper took a moment to appreciate what an attractive couple they were before moving on to admire the sexy yet simple pink dress Chloe was sporting.

Piper: I love this! Damn you, Chloe. Now I have to order this one too!"

"With what money?" Her more logical and less trivial part questioned.

Chloe: Don't blame me. I plan to buy a few more things as well. I already got Talia and Tina five additional customers that want to order that dress.

Piper: Yeah. Lish plans to order from them also. Giving away the clothes to a select group was a brilliant idea.

Chloe: Brilliant minds run in the Fosters blood.

Piper: Hell yeah, it does.

The enthusiastic reply was more than a response to her cousin; it was a reminder to herself. She was a Fosters, which meant that things would work out for her; anything less was unacceptable.

She was intelligent, beautiful, and working towards her goals in life. Soon enough, she would be making enough money to get back to enjoying the finer things, but for right now, she needed to get back to work.

The lasagna sheets were pissing her off as they kept folding in on themselves. Piper had followed the directions to the letter, but there was no mention of what to do with these damn unruly sheets.

Taking a fork, Piper moved with care and precision to straighten the sheet out. Moving too fast with the last three had caused them to tear. It shouldn't matter because it would blend in and be eaten just the same, but she wanted to make the dish look picture perfect.

This one was not going to get the best of her. It would

stay intact and look exactly the way it did when the woman in the apron on the video prepared them.

"Slowly, slowly," she coached herself while moving the fork into the sheet opening and starting to lift.

Then there was a knock on the door, and she pulled up too fast and, of course, broke the sheet again.

"Stupid sheet," Piper said, dropping the fork.

"IT'S OPEN," she yelled in the direction of the door.

Right on time, Daya entered with Jake. The boy barely said hello to Piper before taking off in the direction of the TV.

"Hey, Jake!" Piper yelled. "When you come back next week. I will no longer have cable, so you better enjoy yourself tonight."

Jake gave her a thumbs up and turned on the TV.

"That went better than I expected," Piper said.

Daya laughed.

"That's because he didn't hear a word you said. That reaction was purely him going through the motions so he could get to the fun. When he comes by next week, and there is no TV, he will lose it. But don't worry, I will pack him some extra games."

"I won't have cable, but I still have other stuff we can do."

"That works. He watches too much TV as it is."

Daya moved closer to Piper and gently touched her on the shoulder.

"Is there something I can help with? I haven't had the money to start paying you back yet, but I could skip out on some items for Jake this month and give it to you instead."

Piper shook her head. She had no doubts that Daya would do exactly that. However, like Piper, the young single mom standing before her was having a hard time making ends meet.

"No. Anything extra you have, save it for Jake. I'm sure he

is going to need new clothes and shoes soon. He's growing fast, and the pants he wore last week were a little short."

Daya looked down at her shoe. The embarrassment was easy to see.

"Hey, Daya, it's okay. You are doing a great job."

"I don't know about that, but I am doing the best I can."

"And anyone who says differently is lying."

Daya smiled, pleased at the compliment. Peeping around Piper, she asked, "What are you doing?"

"I was trying to make lasagna, but the sheets keep getting the best of me. If the next sheet eludes me, I'm going to give up and pop it in the oven as is. Poor Jake is going to be my test subject."

"Well, keep in mind that the boy enjoys food. So, if he sings your culinary praises, I wouldn't go entering any cooking contest if I were you. I gave him a plain rice cake the other day to get him to stop hounding me for five minutes, and he said he loved it. If I want lasagna, I buy the frozen kind. Why didn't you do that?"

Piper dropped another sheet into the baking pan. This time it lay flat and perfect. She felt proud.

"I wanted to do something different."

"Yeah, right. I'll bet you're practicing so you can one day become an amazing wife to Scott," she teased.

Piper laughed and tried not to show how much the comment hurt. The only person she had told about her breakup with Scott was Lish.

Daya checked the time and sighed.

"Time to go. You know where to reach me if Jake does anything crazy like gets hurt performing a stunt he saw on TV or if he almost burns your apartment down."

"I do indeed," Piper said, adding a second layer of cheese.

Daya kissed Jake, said a final goodbye to Piper, and left for work. However, Piper didn't hear Daya because she was in a zone, and after adding one last layer of sauce and mozzarella cheese, she opened the oven door and slid her meaty masterpiece inside.

Next, she stood back to admire it through the oven glass. The excitement of making her first adult meal from scratch was too much to keep to herself, so she called Lish.

"Guess what?" Piper announced.

"Aliens kidnapped you, and you're calling me from their spaceship," Lish said.

"Always with the jokes. No. I, Piper Fosters, have just made lasagna from scratch."

Lish gasped.

"Aliens really did kidnap you, and they've already altered your mind! You hate cooking."

"Hate is a strong word. Never interested in it, sounds better."

"Call it what you will, but I'm thrilled for you. I hope it turns out great."

"Me too. Jake is over tonight, so he will be the first to test it."

"Poor Jake."

"Oh, whatever. If it's good, you're going to want some too."

"You're right. May as well save me a slice so that I can try it. I'll pick it up tomorrow when I bring you your gift."

"Gift?"

"Yes. I am delivering a lovely lady giftset to my amazing best friend. It includes fabulous body butters, candles, nail polishes, and even hair removal creams because I am sure on your budget you have not been keeping up with the forest."

The thoughtfulness of her friend's gesture squeezed at Piper's heart.

"You're the best, Lish."

"I know. But you can applaud my wonderful ways tomorrow. I have to go right now. Save me some lasagna," Lish said before ending the call.

Piper looked over at Jake. The TV still had all his attention. Glancing back at the oven, the feeling of achievement surged through her yet again. What meal could she conquer next?

Checking under the cabinets, Piper located a few unopened cooking gadgets. A waffle maker, rice cooker, and air fryer were all purchased that one time Piper was struck with the inspiration to become an at-home chef. Since none were used, it was no surprise that the mood was fleeting.

Piper removed them from their boxes and lined them up on the counter. Maybe tomorrow she could make waffles for breakfast and something simple with rice for lunch.

Her phone beeped with a message from Scott, and just like that, her cheerful spirit became a cautious one.

Scott: It's been a bad day, and I miss you.

Piper's finger hovered over the keyboard. No, she wouldn't do it. If every time Scott needed her during this break, she went running, then this mess would never get sorted out.

Silencing the phone, she picked up the empty boxes and decided now would be a great time to take out the trash.

"I feel like you are timing your trash dumping just to see me," came a voice from behind her.

She pushed a box into the garbage chute and spun around to smile at Desmond. This smile was genuine, unlike the others she had plastered on for the past few days. It was always enjoyable seeing him. He somehow made her feel lighter.

"Don't flatter yourself. I'm pretty sure it's the other way around."

"You're probably right." He looked down at the last flattened box beside her foot with the image of a rice cooker on it.

"I assume you like to cook?"

"You'd be wrong, but it's time I learned. Do you?"

"I'm a good cook, or at least I think I am since Dagger is always trying to get my plate."

"I trust Dagger's judgment. How'd you learn?"

"Cooking classes mostly. I have a friend that's a chef. I attend his classes a few times a month to be supportive. He's got a talent for it and has effectively taught me a thing or two."

" I need a friend like that."

"You're welcome to go with me one day if you'd like."

That sounded dangerous. Being huddled up near Desmond was asking for trouble, but she didn't want to sound dismissive, so she gave the first response to pop into her head.

"I'll think about it."

"He gave her a knowing look and smiled. It was one of those panty-wetting smiles.

"No, you won't, but that's okay. What are you cooking tonight?"

"Lasagna," she answered.

Her mind was still stuck on how effortlessly he had just called her out. Was her lying that obvious? Unexpectedly, Desmond didn't seem upset about it, and damn it, that made him even hotter.

"That sounds good. I love lasagna."

Piper nodded and was about to offer him a plate to make up for her blatant lie when her apartment door swung open.

Both she and Desmond instinctively turned.

"Miss Piper, I went to the bathroom and found this funny-looking thing. What is it?"

She squinted at the object Jake was so casually twirling around in his hands. It was pink, small, and shaped like a . . .

Oh shit, that's my rose vibrator!

Piper completely forgot that it was left in the bathroom on the counter after her solo shower action this morning. Thank goodness she always cleaned it after each use. However, she still wanted Jake to wash his hands . . . a lot.

"Nice chatting with you, Desmond, gotta go," she tossed over her shoulder.

She abandoned the last box and did the fastest walk/run to her apartment ever. Jake was still turning the rose around and inspecting it.

"What is it?" Jake asked again curiously.

"It's an umm . . . an umm . . . air freshener," she said, taking it from his hands and shutting the door.

CHAPTER 3

Piper turned the key in the ignition, and nothing.

"Dammit, I do not need this right now!"

Her morning had already been a rocky storm when it was supposed to have been smooth sailing. Today was the day of her anticipated interview. When she went to sleep last night, good spirits and excitement filled her dreams.

Then around 4 a.m., her dreamy day turned to dread. Her cousin, Russell, called with the news that Aunt Delores had slipped into a diabetic coma. The chances of a positive outcome were slim. After that, Piper could no longer sleep and spent two hours sobbing, hurt, and unsettled.

Finally, she mustered up the energy to prepare for her interview, then this happened. It would be one of those trying days again. Shouldn't she be accustomed to this by now?

Glancing at her cellphone, she began to feel frantic. If she didn't leave within the next ten minutes, she would be late, and that could not happen. This job was perfect; great pay, perks, and best of all, no cleaning out animal cages. She loved the animals at the clinic, but it was time to love them from somewhere else.

Preferably, in a quiet office, at Juniper, where every day was like one of her medical dramas. Nurses rushing around sharing outlandish, jaw-dropping experiences would be fantastic.

Entertaining stories aside, though, Piper wanted and needed this job. She hadn't worked her ass off in school, while stripping for four years, to fail when things got rough.

Turning the key again, Piper got the same result and cursed. She pressed the button to pop the hood and got out to look, unsure of what exactly she was even looking for. Her knowledge about engines wasn't vast, but she assumed the battery was dead since nothing was responding, which was weird because she'd gotten a new battery not too long ago.

Inspecting it didn't confirm anything; the battery looked normal. Then again, did a dead battery look . . . well, dead? Shouldn't it have dried white stuff at the top?

"I'm so fucking clueless," she mumbled to herself.

"I wouldn't say that," Desmond said, coming up behind her.

"Oh, hi," Piper said not too enthusiastically. "How's your morning?"

"I'll go out on a limb and say better than yours. I was bringing some stuff down to my truck before work. What's going on with the car?"

"Absolutely nothing is going on with it. It won't start, and it's being a piece of shit at the worst time."

"You mind if I help? Your battery is probably dead."

"Have at it."

She thought he would step forward and look under the hood, but instead, he told her he would be right back. He went to his truck, and returned holding a medium-sized thick black case.

"What's that?"

"It's a portable jump starter."

Piper browns lifted.

"That little case is used to jump-start cars? I really have been living under a rock. I thought you needed cables hooked up to another car."

Desmond chuckled as he opened the case.

"It can still be done that way, but this is simpler and faster."

"I like faster. I have an interview I am running late for."

"Don't worry, Piper. I got you."

Desmond hooked up the clamps to the battery terminal and pressed a small red button on the device.

Piper couldn't resist. She took a moment to enjoy the view of his tall, muscular body leaning over her car. He was wearing workout clothes that hung and hugged in all the right places.

"Okay, go give it a try."

She rushed to the seat and cranked the car. This time, it roared to life, and Piper sighed with relief.

"Desmond. Thank you so much! You really don't know how much you've helped me."

"Happy to do it."

He removed the clamps and closed the hood while Piper settled into the car. Walking around to the still open car door, Desmond offered her the jumper case.

"Why are you giving me this?"

"Your battery may be fine, but just in case, I don't want you to get stuck anywhere."

She shook her head.

"I'll figure something out if it happens again."

"No, you won't." He tossed the case onto the passenger seat. "It would bother me all day if you got stranded, and I could have prevented it. You can return it whenever."

There was no time for debating. Picking up the case and flipping it over, she said, "I don't even know how to use it."

"All you have to do is turn it on and clamp it to the battery. Red for positive and black for negative. Once the clamps are connected, press the red button, and start the car."

She could only stare at him, overwhelmed by his benevolence—first the gift card, now this.

"All this kindness is going to have me like putty in your hands."

"That's the plan," he said, giving her another one of those panty-dropping smiles.

Closing her car door, Desmond stepped back.

"Good luck on your interview, Piper," he said and walked away.

She wasted another few seconds watching him walk away and then got her head in the game. An interview was calling her name.

The interview went well, or at least that was the impression she received. There was a team of managers firing off questions like they were at an oral shooting range. A lot of what they wanted to know seemed repetitive.

They merely asked the same questions in different ways in an attempt to trip her up, but it wouldn't work. She'd had a hell of a morning and forced herself to turn the sadness over her aunt's current status into a strength she could draw from.

This job isn't only for me. It's for you Aunt Delores. She chanted in her mind throughout the interview.

Therefore, as they tossed them out, Piper answered every

question poised with confidence and ease, delivering the professional, mundane response they expected.

The team thanked her for her time, promising to be in touch, and she went about her merry way, sure that good news was in her future. Her belief in good things happening solidified when the car started with no fuss, causing a flash-back to Desmond.

He did more than necessary and deserved a significant gesture as a thank you. Maybe when she finally felt confident in one of the recipes, she could make it for him and drop it off.

Hitting the button to speed dial her best friend, Piper wasted no time once Lish answered.

"Lish, I kicked ass at my interview!"

"I expected nothing less. Did they ask you any of the questions we practiced?"

"Practically all of them. Thank you so much for helping me out. When I get this job, I want to take you to dinner."

"Ooh somewhere fancy?"

"The fancier, the better."

"I definitely hope you get this job then."

Piper giggled as she pulled to a stoplight and glanced at her reflection in the mirror. She still looked super profes-sional. Her light cherry lipstick was fresh, her stylish curls were still balancing the fine line between messy but classy, and her flawless mocha complexion remained glamorous.

"I feel good, Lish. I finally see the possibility for the life I've always wanted for myself."

"It's not like you haven't worked hard. You will get there."

"Let's hope so. Do you know I almost missed the inter-view because my battery was dead?"

"So, how'd you get there?"

"Desmond."

She could hear her friend perk up, "Say what now?"

"Desmond helped me out by jump-starting my car."

"Did he jump-start anything else?"

"It's not like that."

"Yeah, but you want it to be. Too bad he has a girl."

"And I have a guy, remember? Well, sort of."

"Are you talking about Scott? When was the last time you even spoke to him?"

"It's only been a little over a week."

"And it should be forever, talking about he kissed the nanny because she's crazy. I don't buy it."

"I don't know what I think, but lately, it's like you have all the answers."

Lish laughed.

"Nope, I'm as clueless as always, and it's easier to judge when you're on the outside looking in. If it were me and I were in love with him, he'd probably be back in my bed by now. So, hats off to you for holding out."

"Don't give me any kudos. I feel weak. All this time apart, and I have no answers about the relationship. I miss him but don't know if I trust him."

"I don't like him hurting my friend, and that makes me not the best person to ask for advice. Go with your gut."

"And that's why I love you."

"Love you too."

A few minutes after Piper got off the phone with Lish, it lit up again. Speak of the devil. It was a message from Scott, two to be exact. Piper ignored them until she pulled into a parking spot at home.

The first one was the usual. I love you. I miss you, can I come to see you when I'm in town? That one Piper could ignore, but the second text made her eyes tear up. It was a picture of him and Ryan.

Piper hit the steering wheel. He wasn't playing fair.

How can I say no now?

After further consideration, she concluded that maybe seeing him would be a good thing. It could provide some clarity.

Or add confusion.

Likely the latter but being at a crossroads implied that something had to change. Texting back that one dinner and one dinner only would be acceptable, Piper waited for his response. Before receiving his answer, she quickly added that they could meet at a restaurant and not her place.

If he got her behind closed doors, all her willpower would vanish.

Scott: Thank you. I love you so much.

Piper's response was transparent and happy.

Piper: I love you too and bring that cute baby!

Scott: I sure will.

She got out of the car, remembering to bring Desmond's kit, and walked into the building. Two little kids were playing a game of tag while their mom checked the mail. Piper went over to the organized metal mailboxes lining the wall and did the same.

Climbing the stairs to the second floor, Piper spotted her grumpy neighbor's door wide open. He was sitting on his couch staring at what she assumed was the TV broadcasting a commercial about denture cream.

"Hi, Mr. Leo."

His face tightened as he looked at her through his door-way. Picking up his cane on the side of the couch, he used it to slam the door shut.

"Such a sweet old man," Piper said, smiling to herself.

Walking further down the hall, Piper stopped in front of Desmond's door and knocked. After a few seconds, sounds could be heard from the other side right before it swung open.

There stood Desmond, shirtless and sweaty with a towel tossed over his shoulder.

"Hey, Piper."

"Hi," she said, trying to keep her eyes locked with his so that they couldn't roam anywhere else.

"Did I catch you at a bad time?"

"No, I was only working out. What's up?"

Something dawned on her, and she had to ask.

"I'm surprised you are home. Didn't you say you were heading to work when you helped me this morning?"

"I did, but my client canceled."

"Client, huh? Someone's important."

"Hardly. I'm a personal trainer."

"Oh," she said, unable to stop her eyes from enjoying the view any longer."

He waited until her eyes glided back up and met his before grinning. Embarrassed about being caught in the act, she offered him the black case.

He didn't reach for it.

"Are you sure you don't need to keep it longer?"

Maybe she did, but she wasn't going to.

"No, everything is fine. My car started with no problems."

"Uh-huh, and did you get a new battery yet?"

Piper looked around.

"No, but I will."

"Great, how about you keep it until you do."

"Desmond, I can't—"

"Piper. You have no idea when your battery is going to give out on you again. I don't want you to get stuck anywhere. Until you have a new battery, just keep it. It will make me feel better."

She shrugged and tucked the case into her purse. He'd made a good argument and didn't seem to be interested in budging.

"Thanks again, Desmond. If you need anything from me, such as help moving some boxes, I'm your girl."

"There's no need for that. I'm good."

"You sure? Look at these muscles," Piper joked, flexing her arm.

Desmond laughed and licked his lips.

Oh, to be those lips . . . Stop it!

"Alright. Thank you for going above and beyond your civic duty. I'll let you get back to your workout."

He leaned against the door frame, clearly not ready for the conversation to end.

"Really? How so?"

"Providing me with the jump was one thing, but you didn't have to give me the case too."

"Piper," he said, pausing before moving on. His voice was so deep and assertive, not only her ears, but her body pulsated. "How'd your interview go?"

Oh yeah, her interview. She thought he was about to ask her to come inside and get naked. Truth be told, she wasn't sure the answer would have been no. It was that damn sweaty hard chest and those deep-set eyes, the wavy black hair and monstrous bulge in his pants making it hard to oppose him.

"Um, I think it went great. They interrogated me, I interrogated them, and then the entire painful dance was over."

He nodded slowly. "Good."

He had to have been thinking something. It was there in his eyes, but he said nothing more.

"I have to get home. It's still early in the day, but I need to figure out dinner and get ready for work tomorrow."

She turned to leave, but he stopped her.

"That comment about dinner just reminded me. There is something you can do for me."

Yes, yes. I'll be your dinner. You can lay me down on your table and have first and second helpings of me.

"What's that?" she asked.

"Remember I told you I have a friend that's a chef?"

"Yes, I do."

"He wants me to come to another class to help fill the room. The person originally going with me had to cancel. Do you think you can go instead? Don't worry, it's not a date."

Damn, that was a letdown. But why? She had Scott.

"I can do that. When is it?"

"Saturday at three."

Piper mentally checked her calendar. Nope, nothing on Saturday. There was dinner with Scott on Friday, but that shouldn't also lead to time with him on Saturday. The goal was to take it slow.

"Sounds good."

She said goodbye and spent the next 20 minutes in her apartment daydreaming about sex with Desmond, only to force those thoughts aside to think about sex with Scott.

Scott was the only man she should be lusting after, that is until she officially decided their relationship was over.

Scenes from the first time Scott had his way with her at the club caused a seductive smile to cross her lips. Getting turned on by the memory, Piper reached for her vibrator on a small table next to her bed.

To her dismay, the whole mood got ruined when she heard Vince yell, "Put it in your pooper!" through the wall.

Yup, mood killed.

CHAPTER 4

Piper took special care getting dressed Friday night. A purple fitted skirt, with a soft white V-neck shirt and sexy black heels, were her fashion weapon of choice. It was the first time she would see Scott since their break, and he needed to drool over her even if she wouldn't allow him to have her.

For an extra special touch, Piper grabbed the gold bracelet he'd gifted her three months into their relationship and put it on before heading out the door.

She made it to the restaurant at exactly 6:30 and had no trouble locating Scott and Ryan. When the hostess asked her if she would be dining alone, Piper pointed in the direction of the child, screaming his lungs out, and said, "I'm with them."

Scott didn't see her approach. He was too busy wrestling with an angry baby Ryan who had his mind set on playing with the forks and spoons.

"Hi, Scott."

He looked up, and so did Ryan, and both he and the baby froze. However, Piper was certain it was for two different reasons. Scott, more so consumed by naughty thoughts, and Ryan wondered if the new nice lady would help him finally score those utensils.

Piper reached out towards Ryan, and the baby immediately tried to get to her.

"Piper, you look amazing," Scott said, kissing her on the cheek and passing the baby to her.

"Thanks, you look handsome as well."

Turning her face to brush noses with Ryan, she added, "And so do you, big boy. I missed you."

The boy grinned and then stuck three fingers in his mouth. He then proceeded to touch Piper's face with those newly saturated fingers. Piper didn't mind as she welcomed the kisses and hugs she had so deeply missed from the precious baby.

They sat back down, and Scott watched her with Ryan quietly for a few moments before getting up the courage to say more.

"I am so sorry I hurt you, Piper."

Piper was bouncing the baby on her leg and avoiding eye contact with Scott. She didn't want to look at him, especially into his eyes. The softness and warmth in them would ruin her. Hell, who was she kidding? Being near him made the weight of their separation so heavy Piper felt weak in the knees.

"You did but, I'm working through it."

"Will *we*," he said, emphasizing the word, "be able to work through it?"

Piper ignored his question and asked one of her own.

"What's going on with Simone?"

"I'm narrowing down a way to get rid of her. It shouldn't be too much longer, and then she disappears out of our lives for good."

Something about the way he said that didn't sit right

with her. But how much comfort should she expect in a conversation about him and the woman he locked lips with.

Still avoiding eye contact, Piper said, "You make it sound so final. I know you said she is crazy. Are you trying to get her sent to an institute without her knowing?"

"Something like that. More so than anything, I've been working desperately to locate a replacement, and I think I have found one that looks promising."

Scott smiled and tried again to make eye contact with her, but Piper focused on the salt shaker instead. A waitress came over to provide them with menus and drop off two glasses of water and a kid's cup for Ryan, which he dove towards immediately and began swinging it, getting splashes of water on Piper's face.

"You want me to take him?"

Hell no!

Ryan was offering her an out. A way to keep a sort of wall up between them. Piper would hold this little boy throughout dinner and eat with one hand if necessary.

Plus, she missed him, and the innocent smiles and gurgles offered Piper a comfort that she didn't even know she needed. Hopefully, kids were in her future, but did she want those kids to be with Scott?

"No, I'm good."

"Alright," he said slowly, "but you've barely looked at me."

"I looked at you."

"Piper, that's bullshit. If you won't look at me, will you at least answer my question?"

"What question?"

"About us. Can we work through this?"

"Let's just get through dinner?"

He reached across the table and touched her, and instinctively, her eyes shifted to his.

"I have been trying to give you your space, but I miss you, and I love you. What can I do to make this right?"

His touch was delicate; his eyes were sincere, and his voice so kind. Piper took hold of his hand.

"I've missed you too, Scott."

Her strength and ability to resist him fled her body like she'd been holding it hostage these past couple of weeks. Staying away from the man she loved had been trying but now that they were here, together, and happy, working things out felt right.

They finished dinner and went back to her place. Ryan fell asleep, and they spent the rest of the night getting reacquainted in a way that Piper had deeply missed.

The following morning, he left to drop Ryan off at his grandparent's and complete his own tasks while in town.

After he kissed her goodbye, two questions came to mind about two different men. Could she trust one? And could she trust herself around the other?

Desmond looked delicious, and that was not a compliment. It was a complaint. A complaint that was causing trouble and confusion within her brain and body.

Why couldn't he simply look ordinary? Be ordinary? Instead of a gentleman wrapped in temptation.

Piper had been attracted to many men over her short life but never at such depths while in love with another. On second thought, which was too late now, attending this class with him may not have been such a great idea.

"Are you ready?" he asked, standing in her doorway, so tall his head almost touched the top of it. He was wearing tan slacks and a navy-blue button-down shirt.

"Sure. You want me to drive?" she offered.

"No, you can ride with me?"

He held the truck door open for her and helped her inside. Once he got in, they were on their way.

"How long have you been a personal trainer?"

"For three years. Before that, I was a physical therapist for the NFL."

"The Pros, huh? I can see it. You definitely have the body for it. Do you miss it?"

"Not really, the players carried a whole lot more stress than the physical. I think having the name therapist in my title meant a lot of them unloaded their personal issues onto me."

"Ahh, yeah, that would suck."

"It wasn't always bad. It just got old. Changing up my clientele made a difference. And you? What did you dabble in before your love of animals."

"I was a stripper," Piper replied with her usual nonchalance.

"Really? I've dated a few strippers, not to mention strip clubs took all of my money during my college years."

"Good for them," Piper said proudly.

"Are you kidding?" Desmond laughed. "You have no sympathy for the horny wide-eyed, 19-year-old that spent all of his money?"

"Not at all. It's the stripper's oath. I don't have to be one to always cheer them on."

"That's fair. I enjoyed every minute of it anyway. Why did you stop?"

"It was fun during the time, but that's not the job I wanted forever. I also had an aunt that I promised I'd switch the path of my life. So, I went to college, got a degree, and relocated from a pole to a desk."

She hadn't even told Scott that part of the reason stripping was over had a lot to do with Aunt Delores. The words fell out, and it caught her by surprise. Desmond was simply easy to talk to.

"That's pretty cool."

"You mean because I gave up stripping?"

"I mean taking control of your life to do what makes you happy, whatever that may be. It requires guts, and I'm sure your aunt is proud."

"Yeah, well, now I'm rethinking it. Stripping paid a lot more than my current job does."

"Don't give up. You'll get through the rough patch."

His encouraging words were sweet and yet another thing that made him sexy.

"I was kidding about going back to stripping."

And she was . . . mostly.

"It wouldn't surprise me if you weren't. I felt the same way when I initially switched positions. The pay cut was drastic, but I found my footing and increased my income after a while. Even if I hadn't, my happiness was more important."

"If that didn't work out, you could have always considered being a stripper."

"Ha, I doubt anyone would want to see me shake my ass."

Piper begged to differ, but she didn't comment. She truly enjoyed his sense of humor. It dawned on her that she didn't laugh a lot like this with Scott. There were humorous comments here and there, but it was different, and Scott wasn't what one would call funny.

"What do you like to do?" Piper asked.

"Build drones and model cars, workout, and spend time with family."

"You're so much more mature than me. How old are you?"

"Thirty-one, and I've had my extremely wild days. Been

arrested, woke up a few times not knowing what happened the night before more times than I care to share, and as you know, wasted all my money on strippers. Now I'm a responsible dog owner who supports his friends and tries to give others the small bit of wisdom I've picked up."

"See so noble. I'm only 26 and I don't build anything, but I like buying things. As well as visiting spas, painting and watching medical TV dramas."

"But you're doing great. Did you want to be a doctor at some point?"

"No, I can't handle all the blood in real life, but what the human body can endure and keep on ticking is nothing short of amazing."

"When I catch something gross on TV, I will be sure to let you know."

"You could always be grossed out with me," Piper said, offering him the invite before thinking it through.

He stole a quick glance at her.

"If you invite me, I'm there."

Arriving at the cooking class, Desmond introduced Piper to his friend, William, the evening chef. William was a tall, heavy-set guy with a contagious laugh. He and Desmond had been friends since they were ten and had countless stories about their fun, highly competitive childhoods.

William jokingly admitted he still resented Desmond for winning his car in a football bet, even though Desmond returned it to him a few weeks later.

"It's very nice meeting you, Piper. Thanks for coming. I know it must be hard having to deal with Desmond for long periods."

"I'm sure the delicious food we are making tonight will make up for."

"A woman that loves food. Keep her close, Desmond. I might try to steal her away."

Before Piper or Desmond could correct him, on the assumption that they were an item, someone called his name, and William excused himself.

"Sorry about that," Desmond said. "He doesn't know we are only friends."

Piper smiled, not trusting any words to leave her mouth. Her brain was going into overdrive.

How did William not know that I'm not Desmond's girlfriend? Didn't he say they were friends since they were 10 years old? Unless I misunderstood and they aren't close friends? But that doesn't seem to fit either. The only other answer would be that Desmond doesn't have a girlfriend. Or not one he told William about.

This could all be solved if Piper simply asked Desmond if he had a girlfriend, but that was none of her business, and it made no difference. Scott was her man.

Desmond led her to an oversized, spotless kitchen island with a sink. There were 10 of those island-style cooking stations in the room—five on one side and another five on the other. The only item on the counter was a cream-colored 5X7 card with 'necessary items for tonight's meal' written at the top.

"I'm warning you, I can barely cook, so don't trust me with anything significant."

"You're in good and hands," Desmond assured her.

He picked up the card and handed it to her.

"We can start setup. Tell me what tools we will need, and I'll get them."

"I can do that."

She cleared her throat and recited everything under the

tools section of the list while Desmond collected them from the cabinet underneath their station.

"Alright," Desmond said after he had placed the last piece on top. "What are we cooking tonight?"

Piper scanned the card.

"I don't see it, but the meal includes chicken and beef."

"Flip it over, it's on the back."

After doing so, the words 'Chicken and Beef Stir Fry' were easily visible in big, bold letters.

"Aren't you the smart one?"

"I've been here a couple of times, remember? We got about five minutes until the class starts."

Piper was studying the 'how to prepare' section of the menu card.

"Great. That's just enough time for you to explain to me the differences between Steam, Grill, Sear, Braise, Poach, Roast, and," she squinted at the smaller words grouped at the bottom of the card. "Blanch?"

"You don't waste any time."

"Nope. They are listed right here as the seven cooking methods, and I have only ever heard of three of them."

Desmond took the card and pointed to the first word, providing a detailed yet straightforward explanation to Piper's question. By the time he was done with all seven, the class was beginning.

The entire cooking experience was phenomenal. William was brilliant, talented, and so much more than a chef; he was a culinary artist. The way he performed those magical moves with his wrist that sent the vegetables into the air before they gracefully dove back into the pan was highly skillful.

All his instructions to the class were clear, to the point, and easy to follow. He even tossed in a few jokes making the entire group laugh several times.

There was so much knowledge, confidence, and passion

about cooking gained from the class that Piper hoped she could one day return. William had no idea of the courage in cooking this night had provided for Piper. Having a better grasp of seasonings, food temperatures, and portion sizes made a considerable difference in her enthusiasm level.

When the night was over, Desmond walked her to her front door. Mr. Leo shot them a bird as they went by, and they both had a good laugh.

"Thanks for coming with me, Piper."

"Thanks for inviting me. It was fun," she lifted the brown paper bag, "and I have leftovers."

"You're quite welcome."

He brushed her chin lightly with his hand.

"Enjoy your night, sweetie."

Then he was gone, and so was Piper, inside to masturbate to the hot idea of a spicy night with Desmond.

Piper's alarm jerked her out of sleep and a good dream Monday morning. This time it was about Scott, and he was telling her all the reasons she was the woman he wanted to marry. They were happy on a tranquil beach, and Ryan was returning all of his Daiquiris for bottles of milk.

After getting dressed for work and with 10 minutes to spare, Piper grabbed her purse and headed to her car. Today felt like a good day, and even though things might be rocky in her life, everything would work out. She and Scott were back on decent terms, and there was a great friendship developing between her and Desmond.

Reaching inside for her keys, her hand grazed the jumper case he had loaned her. Getting a new battery was at the top of her list when extra money came in. Desmond was a nice guy, and he didn't deserve some indigent, hopeless friend.

Piper pressed the button to unlock her car and stopped. A new car battery was the last thing Piper needed to worry about because in front of her was a car that sported four flat tires.

CHAPTER 5

"Did you get my gift?" Simone asked.

Piper was so angry she literally saw red. No wait, that was blood, her blood.

When the call from Simone came in, Piper was cutting vegetables. She answered through her Bluetooth, which meant she didn't check the caller ID, a mistake that wouldn't happen again.

As soon as Simone's voice sounded in her ear, Piper pressed down on the knife without appropriately ensuring her fingers were in the clear. Thankfully the cut was not life-threatening, but she should get it cleaned up.

"Yeah, I got your gift. Why don't you come over and let me thank you in person?"

The woman cackled.

"Oh, Piper, I'm not stupid, you are. I told you to back off or else, but you just wouldn't listen. You're a stubborn girl, I see. I'm going to have to teach you some manners."

"We will see how funny you think this is when my fist connects to your mouth. Why are you hiding behind a phone anyway? If you're so bold, show yourself."

Piper hadn't been in a fight since high school. Outside of the close call at Tina's party, keeping her temper in check was preferable and usually possible. However, in this case, an exception could be made.

"In due time. Not to mention it's more fun this way. Ruining your life from a distance and sitting back and watching it crumble. I'll bet now you'll think twice about messing with Scott."

"This is so not about him right now. You've crossed the line and damaged my property. Fuck Scott, this is between you and me."

"Aww, you're so cute when you're mad, and since I'm a nice girl, I'll tell you once more. BACK OFF!"

"MAKE ME!"

"You're going to regret not taking my offer."

Piper tried to remind herself that the girl was immature, crazy, and would be out of Scott's life soon, but Piper wanted revenge now regardless of Simone's expiration date.

"First and foremost, Simone, I don't know who—"

"Why the fuck are you calling me Simone?"

"Because that's your name, is it not?"

Piper could hear the woman on the phone release a twisted cold smirk.

"You're so dumb. He tells you anything, and you go for it. Don't worry about my name. Just know that I know your name. And you've been warned."

Then she ended the call.

Piper continued to stand in front of her kitchen island, blazing with fury. The audacity of this woman threatening her, destroying her things, and expecting Piper to cower and run away, not going to happen.

But what was that comment about her name not being Simone? Wasn't she Scott's nanny?

It now seemed foolish that in all this time, why hadn't

she asked to meet the lady taking care of Ryan? For that matter, why hadn't Scott offered to introduce them some time ago?

Things weren't adding up, and the more she trusted Scott, the trickier their relationship became, and to her consternation, there was no off switch to stop loving him.

It seemed Lish was correct—abandonment issues were a trait she carried around. Giving up on Scott felt cold and hypocritical. He was going through a rough time which meant he needed her to get closer, not run further away.

But how could she stay in his corner if she had no idea about the secrets that lurked there? If she was going to stick around, she needed answers.

Unlocking her phone, Piper hit the button to call Scott and waited for it to connect to her Bluetooth.

Next, she took the knife and went over to the sink to run some cold water on her bloody finger. A quick examination showed that the cut wasn't deep, and a small bandaid should suffice for protection.

As the phone rang in her ear, Piper half expected it to go to voicemail. Scott rarely ever answered the phone during his work hours. When she heard his voice on the other line, she stood straighter.

"Hey, Piper."

"I thought you were getting rid of her?"

"Who?"

"Simone! Who else would I be talking about?"

Piper heard movement on his end, and then a door closed.

"I asked who because I've already told you I'm getting rid of her. I didn't understand why you would be asking me such a stupid question."

"STUPID?" Piper yelled, staring down at the knife.

As easily as it had cut her finger, slicing through two

bodies should be a piece of cake. Simone was already on the list; Scott was welcome to join in.

"Who in the hell are you talking to, Scott?"

"Piper, calm down. I'm joking."

"This is nothing to joke about. Your lunatic nanny has flattened all four of my fucking tires. How in the hell does she even know where I live?"

"Wait. What?"

Piper repeated herself in an angry snippet.

"Tires shredded in my parking lot. How?"

"She must have followed me there or something. Are you sure it was her?"

"Yes, I'm sure. Not only did she call to claim her handy work, but she also threatened that I had more coming if I don't leave you alone."

"Piper, calm down. I told you she was losing it and needed help. I'm getting rid of her soon."

"You may not have to worry about getting rid of her. If I get my hands on her, I'll take care of it."

That was actually a good idea. Piper eyed her purse across the room.

"She's at your house right now, isn't she? I can just pay her a little visit."

"No, you can't."

"And why not?"

"For one thing, four flat tires, remember? Also, Simone isn't there. Ryan is with his grandparents. Simone told me she had to handle an emergency a few days ago."

Piper had forgotten entirely about the flat tires, too occupied with thoughts of retaliation.

"I'll bet she did," Piper commented more to herself than him. "When does she return?"

"No, Piper, you aren't confronting her. Simone needs

professional help, not to be murdered. She is merely a young, naive girl with a crush."

"Yeah, and aren't you just loving it?"

"I'm not. But I did promise you I will handle it, and I will. You are too angry right now, and if you talk to her, things will only worsen."

"But I'm already talking to her. At her choosing anyway. And by the way, today, she said her name isn't Simone. Explain that."

"What do you mean she said her name wasn't Simone?"

"Stop making me repeat myself, Scott!"

"Okay, Okay. What did she say her name was?"

"Why are you asking me? What do you call her?"

"I call her Simone."

"Well, maybe she got it changed," Piper said sarcastically. "Or maybe it's someone else. Got any more women tucked away, Scott?" Piper asked, her voice rising with each word.

"Don't do that, Piper. Don't make accusations and create more issues. There is no one else."

"I'm not doing anything. This is your mess, and now I have to replace tires with money that I don't have. I missed work today, Scott. I can't miss days. "

"I know, Baby I'm sorry."

"I don't need apologies. I need you to get rid of her and replace my tires."

He let out an audible sigh.

"Piper, you know I would help you if I could. I don't have any extra money. Everything extra is going to Ryan, remember?"

Somehow, she knew he would say that. Use the one thing that she couldn't fight him on, resulting in her being left out in the cold yet again to deal with problems independently. Hell, at the rate they were going, she was better off alone.

"Piper. Please don't be mad. I'm doing my best here. I told you this would take time."

"How much time? Last we spoke, you said there was someone you liked."

"There is but, getting the terms right has been tricky. Currently, the woman is unable to do a live-in position."

"This is all so convenient," she said, rolling her eyes.

"Do you think I would put you through this? Put us through this? I love you, and that means something to me. I would do anything for you. Don't worry I'm going to talk to Simone, and she won't bother you again."

"I don't believe you? I wish I did, but I don't. What's going on, Scott?"

"I've gotten myself into a horrible situation is what's going on. I lost my wife, I'm trying to take care of my child, my nanny is threatening the woman I love, and I'm powerless to make you see that I will fix everything. I only need patience."

Tears swelled in her eyes. Whether it was for him, her, or both, she was uncertain. Loving him wasn't easy, and loving him through this nightmare was torturous.

"I can't deal with this right now," Piper said, her words unable to accurately convey the intense level of sadness in her heart.

"I'm not saying I want to leave you, Scott. But maybe we can talk in a few days."

"Stop doing that. Stop backing away from me when things get complicated. That's not how love works. Don't you love me?"

"Yes, I love you, and I'm not backing away. I wouldn't do that to you."

"Then be there for me."

Hearing him say those words hurt.

Have I somehow made him feel like I was emotionally unavailable or didn't care?

If she did, that was never her intention.

"I'm sorry, I can't imagine what you're going through."

"No worries. I know you're also going through a lot. But remember, the rest of the world doesn't matter it's all about you and me."

He said the words with the uttermost sincerity. The silence grew thicker as Piper battled emotions over so many things piling on at once.

"We're a team, and I need you to get through this. I love you, and Ryan loves you."

The nail in the coffin. Her one major weakness, loving someone and having them love her back. Expecting relationships to always be pretty was unrealistic. Scott cared about her, and that made a meaningful difference.

When she was still quiet, he asked in a gentle tone, "Sweetie are you there?"

"I'm here, Scott. There is just a lot going on."

"Like what? Tell me. Talk to me."

"I don't know what to think about all of this. There is so much happening so fast, and I feel like I'm losing you."

"You aren't losing me, Piper, I promise you. If anything, going through tough times together is what makes relationships stronger. I understand this is hard, but you can always call me."

"But you barely answer."

"You know how work can be. I'll always call or text you as soon as I can. Don't I always do that?"

He did. Or at least it seemed like he did.

"I guess you do."

"I do, and I miss you like crazy when I'm not near you. It's going to work out for us. You take care of me, and I'll always take care of you."

"I get that you'll try, but I need tires, and you can't help me at all."

"Is money the only purpose you feel I have? Wow, Piper, I thought we were more than that. The one thing I can't do, and you're going to hold it over my head."

"That's not what I'm doing?"

"Maybe not, but it still cuts deep. Besides, I'm sure there is something you could do. Maybe borrow the money from a friend or . . ."

"Or what?"

"I know you said you never wanted to, but you could return to stripping, couldn't you? At least for a little while if you're having money troubles."

Piper's eyes instinctively closed. Would she ever get away from being a stripper as her only fallback option? Scott seemed to think a quick return was no big deal, while Desmond thought she could overcome her financial woes. Who was right? She knew who she wanted to be. However, the fact remained that good intentions, dreams and wishes didn't pay bills.

"I was hoping I wouldn't have to go back to that," she said softly.

"It's not like it would be forever. You're a strong woman that's what I love about you. Listen, I hate to do this, but I have to go. I will call you back tonight or tomorrow, okay?"

"Yeah."

"I love you, Piper."

"Love you too," she replied after the call ended.

Piper pulled out a chair and sat down, no longer in the mood for the incredible taco salad that made her taste buds water an hour ago. Her phone buzzed again, and she thought twice before hitting her Bluetooth to answer, but decided why not? If it was Simone, maybe this time Piper could get her location.

"Hello?"

"Piper, she's gone."

Those were the first and only words, her cousin Russell said before Piper slumped to the floor.

"When?" she asked so quietly that there was uncertainty if she'd said it at all.

"About an hour ago. I'm trying to be strong. I know she was in a lot of pain."

This was true, and Piper echoed his sentiments, but Aunt Delores was gone, and even though the woman that was like a mother to her finally had the peace she deserved, it still caused Piper great pain.

It felt like her heart was splitting and nothing in the room seemed to be real.

This all has to be a dream. She thought.

However, hearing the soft sniffling coming from Russell on the other end assured her it was not. She stared at the wall, her spirits so low her physical body felt drained. Never in her life had she felt so tired.

"I'll be there as soon as I can, Russell," Piper promised in a quiet voice.

"Thanks Piper," was the last thing he said before freeing her from the call and going back to his own prison of pain.

She'd lost an aunt, but he'd lost a mom, and he would need her right now.

She fell back, lying completely flat on the floor. She had no idea how she would afford to make it to her aunt's funeral. Piper always thought there would be more time and she'd get one last chance to see her aunt, but now it was too late. And the next time she would see Aunt Delores, the woman would be in a casket.

A casket. The thought felt cold and disturbing.

Her aunt didn't belong there, but what one deserved

wasn't always what they got. Dealing with what was, not what could be, was how people survived.

And how will I survive this? She wondered.

If affording cable was out of the question, affording a trip to Miami was inconceivable. The cost would be close to $2,000 once she added in time missed from work, flight tickets, and hotel stay.

Nevertheless, nothing in this world would stop her from going. Her life had become full of choices she didn't want to make. What was one more?

CHAPTER 6

"**A**re you sure you want to do this, Piper?" Lish asked her.

"Since when has what I wanted mattered?"

Lish sighed.

"I know how hard you worked to avoid going backward. I can give you the money, or at least some of it."

"Lish, you paid for the tires; that's enough. I've also calculated costs. It's going to be pricey for me to cover the trip to Miami and bills due to the workdays I will miss."

Piper laced up another boot and then sat down to start her makeup.

"Scott couldn't help?"

"Nope, he has his own money problems."

"Damn. Didn't he get hurt some time ago at work? He should have workers comp coming or something, right?"

"Don't know. Don't care."

"What about your cousins? Chloe? Russell? Talia?"

Piper tapped the brush to shake off any loose powder before applying it.

"Didn't ask."

Excitement flooded Lisa's tone.

"Okay, there you go. I'll bet one of them will help."

Piper stopped and lowered the brush. She looked at Lish through the mirror.

"Give it up. I'm not going to ask them. It's Saturday night, and the crowd looks pretty big out there. If I'm lucky, I can make what I need between tonight and tomorrow."

Lish's shoulders slumped, and she took a step closer to Piper.

"This is hard for me. I feel like I'm the one suffering. I can't imagine what you're going through."

"That's what makes you a great friend and I love you for it, but this battle is mine."

Lish nodded.

"This too shall pass, Piper. I'm going to let you finish preparing. If you need me, I'll be in the bar area."

Then gently moving a lock of hair from Piper's face, she said, "Get em' hard, my dear friend," before bending down to kiss Piper on the cheek.

Piper gave her a grateful smile and finished her makeup.

Fifteen minutes later, it was Piper's turn to take the stage. Instantly she noticed how disconnected and out of place it all felt. Her body moved when the music began, but it did so in a robotic-like state.

Bending, turning, and pulling off articles of clothing in a way that may have made her appear sexy to the audience, even though she felt anything but. Her life was pitiful. Years of school, searching for work, and back exactly where she started.

It was ironic, doing the one thing she'd promised to quit in order to see the one person she'd made the promise to, one final time. The thought made tears sting her eyes, but Piper refused to let them fall.

She would be okay. Isn't that what Desmond had said?

He'd gone through a rough patch too. Rough patches happened, but things could still even out. Thinking of him brought a tiny smile to her lips and eased a bit of the gloom in her heart. She focused on him and their time at the cooking class and made it through the rest of her show.

Piper felt numb the next day as she lay in bed staring at the ceiling and rethinking all her life choices. Her time at the Golden Bar last night proved to be, as she recalled, lucrative. Saturday nights always were. Between the stage time and private shows, her earnings were close to $700.

A good night indeed, but it wasn't enough. Returning tonight could be beneficial, but that wouldn't happen because she wasn't going back.

In the short term, that meant driving to Miami instead of flying, which she should have considered in the first place, but caviar dreams died hard.

In addition, skipping the hotel and asking Russell if she could stay with him and his two male roommates was likely acceptable for him but undesirable for her. The good news was that making these changes meant that she was only two hundred dollars short.

In the long term, not resorting to stripping anymore indicated Piper would need to get a cheaper apartment or take in a roommate, both of which she was willing to do.

The familiar vibration of her phone interrupted her thoughts. It was a message from Scott.

Scott: Hey, Baby. I had some mail sent to your place. If it didn't arrive yesterday, it should be there soon.

Piper: Why would you send mail here without letting me know first?

Scott: I assumed it would be okay.

Piper pushed the button to call him. When he answered, she asked, "What is it? And why are you sending it here again?"

"It's something important from the job that I need when I'm in Georgia. I would have sent it to my house, but I didn't want to risk Simone seeing it. I thought the safest place to send it would be to your place."

Now she felt like an ass. Pressuring him to get rid of Simone, and as soon as he began phasing the woman out, she gave him crap about using her address.

"It's no big deal. Of course, you can use my address. I never checked the mail yesterday. I'll go see if it's there now."

"Thank you, Piper. Are you feeling okay today? I know you're probably thinking about your aunt non-stop."

"I'm pretty good, no complaints," she lied.

"Did you make all the money you needed at the club last night?"

"No," she said, rolling over to face the wall where her dresser stood. From here, she could see the gold bracelet he had given her three months into their relationship. Things were so good then. They had so much fun, and she always felt excited to see him. The excitement was still there, but it had dimmed significantly.

"So, you have to go back tonight?"

"Seems like it."

It was another lie, but what difference did it make? Informing him yet again of her emotional and financially damaged life was futile.

"Great. Alright, babe, I have to get back to work. Love you talk to you soon."

Tossing the phone back onto the bed, she went to freshen up before heading downstairs to check the mail. On the way, Piper almost collided with an overly excited

Vince. He was rushing upstairs past her and waving a package.

"I got my mail order titties," he screamed.

"What the hell?" Piper responded, unsure of what she'd just heard.

Vince had made it to the top of the stairs and almost tripped, trying to make it to his apartment.

Piper made it to the bottom with her brows still drawn and no logical answer coming to mind.

Lacy approached the stairs, and Piper pointed upward, unable to ask a question because there was major uncertainty in what she'd witnessed.

"Don't mind him, Piper. He's excited about a new sex game we have."

Lacy was in her mid-forties, only five feet tall, and likely weighed under a hundred pounds. She had a heavy southern accent and always seemed to be chewing gum. Lacy was super sweet, but to be involved with Vince, she had to be some type of paranormal freak.

"I already hate myself for asking this, but what are mail order titties? And why do they have him so excited?"

Lacy squealed with laughter.

"It's a thriller game where he has to locate which ones are real amongst all the fake ones."

Yup, Piper was regretting that she asked. What Lacy described made no earthly sense. Who wanted to play a breast guessing game? Well, obviously Vince did, but still. Piper's response was to stare at Lacy because she was now more confused than before.

"Okay. I'm not making sense, don't worry, it's confusing for newbies," Lacy said, giving Piper a playful tap on her shoulder.

"So there is a board that the woman holds up. It has 12 circular cut-outs all the same size, she picks the two to place

57

her breast through, and the fake ones go over the other 10 circles. And the guy tries to guess which ones are real."

She concluded her explanation with a smile that said this game was the best one ever invented.

Piper should stop while she was ahead. It was not wise to fall deeper into this rabbit hole of elaborate erotic interests that this couple had concocted, but she had to know.

"Can't he simply touch them to know which ones are real?"

"Oh no, it's against the rules to use his hands. That's the fun part. However, he can rub the nipples with ice cubes, flick his tongue over it, or apply a nipple clamp to the ones he thinks are real. Also, a sheer eye mask is provided to blur the vision."

"That's umm interesting," Piper offered, hiding her disgust.

"Maybe you and your guy should try it?"

"No. That doesn't sound like my style."

Lacy leaned in closer, and Piper could feel the heat of her breath and smell the minty sweetness of the gum she was chewing.

"I know what you're thinking. Why do the men have all the fun? Not true. There is another version where the guy gets to put his dick through the hole on a board filled with 11 other fake dicks. You'd probably like that one better, huh?"

"That's exactly what I was thinking," Piper said. She had to end this madness.

Lacy winked and ran upstairs to join Vince. By now, he was probably licking all the fake breasts for fun.

Piper went over to her mailbox and inserted the key. There were a few bills, pizza coupons, and an envelope for Scott. It was from his employer, Lancer Communications in Milwaukee.

Closing the small square door, Piper locked it and pocketed the tiny key.

Desmond was coming downstairs, with Dagger leading the way. Finally, a face she was happy to see.

"Hi, there," Piper said.

"Hey. What are you up to?"

"Nothing much, grabbing the mail. Are you heading out for a run?"

"Yeah. Running helps me think, which is why I do a lot of it."

"That's a good habit to have."

"Yeah, especially since I won't be able to do it for a few days. Dagger and I are getting ready to go out of town to visit some family."

The mention of family and travel momentarily caused Piper's mind to slip back to her aunt.

Covering the thought, to keep the melancholy emotions at bay, she said, "Aww, that's sweet. When do you leave?"

"This evening."

It wasn't working. The overwhelming sorrow was edging in, and Piper didn't want the inner turmoil to show on her face. Therefore, she wished Desmond a safe trip, patted Dagger on the head, and started to walk away.

"Piper," Desmond said, stopping her. "What's wrong?"

"Nothing."

He crossed his arms and stared at her.

"Now, I don't believe that. Come on, I might have some advice."

"I highly doubt it."

"Humor me anyway."

When Piper didn't say anything, he offered an alternative.

"Tell you what, you don't have to tell me. Instead, you can tell Dagger. He's easy to talk to and good at keeping secrets."

Piper rolled her eyes and smiled in spite of herself, then turned slightly to face the dog.

"Alright, Dagger, I have some financial matters to figure out, have any words of advice?"

Dagger slumped to the floor and looked up at the two of them.

Desmond and Piper laughed.

"Sorry, Piper. I think this topic is not relatable because I pay for his every desire."

"Figures."

"But I did overhear. Maybe you could ask a friend for help?"

Piper thought of Scott's reaction and how small it made her feel. Asking for help was not her forte, and opening up like that again wouldn't happen anytime soon.

"No, not really."

"Oh yeah, you did tell me you don't like asking for help."

"That's true, but everything will work out," she said.

Her comment was nothing more than lip service. Piper wasn't sure of anything anymore.

"Anyway, you two have a safe trip."

"Dammit, you know what? I just remembered. I'm going to be super busy while out of town. So busy I may forget to give Dagger his medicine."

"What medicine?"

"He got another UTI."

"That's horrible. You have to remember to give him his meds. He could get very sick if that doesn't get cleared up. I wonder why it keeps happening?"

"I'm not sure, but the doctors are looking into it. If only I could think of someone to help me out while I go out of town."

Desmond touched his chin as if in deep thought.

"Do you think you could keep him for me? I'll only be gone a few days, and I could pay you for the inconvenience."

She squinted at him.

"Suddenly, you can't take dagger with you?"

"I could," he said slowly, "but it would honestly be easier not to. Can you help me out?"

"I'm not sure. I have to go to work from Monday until Wednesday, and on Thursday, I'm heading out of town myself."

"That's perfect. I will be back on Wednesday, and he doesn't need the medicine until the evenings."

Piper looked at Dagger and then back to Desmond. He had such a handsome face and kind eyes.

What did she have to lose? Keeping Dagger wouldn't be any trouble, and the extra money would help her with the $200 she was short. The more she thought about it, the more the problem was getting solved right before her eyes.

"I can do that," she agreed.

"Thanks. What will you charge me?"

"Uh, I don't know Desmond, whatever works for you is fine. It won't be a lot of work.

"Yes, but it's still an inconvenience. Does $250 sound fair?"

Piper had to blink and force herself not to move so that she didn't jump for joy.

"I think that sounds very fair."

"Good. I'll bring him over in a couple of hours."

"I'll be home." she said excitedly and then added, "Desmond, you didn't have to do this."

"Do what? You're helping me out of a serious bind."

He smiled at her, and then he and Dagger exited the apartment building.

Piper ran upstairs, almost as fast as Vince had earlier. Not only did she no longer have to return to the Golden Bar tonight, but she also now had enough money to attend her aunt's funeral.

When she reached the second-floor landing, there was an odd sound of distant cheering. However, it was unlike any applause she'd heard before because it would only last for a few seconds, go completely quiet and then start up again.

Slowing her steps, it was evident that Vince and Lacy's door was slightly ajar. They must have been so excited about the new toy that they didn't have time to waste shutting the door.

Moving closer, with the intent of doing the neighborly thing and closing it, Piper stopped when she caught a glimpse of movement from inside. It took a few seconds, but eventually, her vision focused on a naked Vince and Lacy.

"Close the door, Piper. Just close the door," she said to herself.

Too bad her mind and hands weren't working as a team. Without question, she should close the door and save her eyes from the need to be sanitized, but it wasn't that simple. Vince had Lacy in the doggy-style position on the kitchen table with a string tied to her ankle.

It connected to a square device located on the floor, and every time he pushed into her, the string would yank on the device, and a round of applause would burst from the small box. Talk about ego-boosting.

Piper had never been so transfixed and disturbed at the same time. Vince's tall body was in pretty good shape for a guy in his late forties. Most of the fat centered around his stomach, where an apparent beer belly had made itself at home. His dick was also pretty striking. What it lacked in length, it made up for in girth.

Lacy was crying out Vince's name like she was angry at him instead of aroused. But Piper quickly understood it was part of their game because Vince demanded that she say it louder and more aggressively.

At one point, Lacy got so loud, Piper had to look over her shoulder to make sure none of the other neighbors had come out of their apartments wondering what all the commotion was.

Vince continued his firm, steady thrusts with the applause exploding almost instantaneously. He slapped Lacy on the ass a few times, and once so hard she almost slipped off the table, but at the last second, he caught her and resumed his motions.

Not long after, they both came in a rush of curses and moans that made Piper want to plug her ears. Assuming she'd seen all the oddities that this couple had to share, she prepared to pull the door shut.

Vince and Lacy were strange to watch, but overall, they weren't too out of the normal. That was until the unthinkable happened. Vince grabbed his still-hard dick and began jumping up and down.

"I have to pee, Lacy. Hurry up!"

"Hold up, sweets, I got you," she said, her southern twang incredibly heavy.

Lacy rushed to the cabinet and grabbed a large, white plastic cup.

Piper's eyes widened.

What the hell?

Lacy held the cup up in front of Vince, and he peed into it. This was indeed one of those train wrecks moments that Piper wished she could look away from, but the mystery of what would happen next held her captive.

Not to mention, her mind was now in agreement with her hands. That this door could not be closed until they saw this through.

Vince finished emptying himself into the cup, and Lacy

lifted it and smiled. At that very second, with the cup aligned to the front of her face, Piper prayed that Lacy didn't do what she thought. The woman had just whispered into her ear downstairs, which meant traces of . . . Piper shuddered, not even wanting to finish the thought.

"Are you ready?" Lacy asked Vince with a naughty smile.

"You know what I like," he said in response.

"If Piper's eyes could have fallen out of her head, that would have been the exact moment that they ejected, leaving her there to figure out her own way home.

Lacy lifted the cup higher and then threw it into Vince's face.

"HELL YEAH!" he shouted as if being splashed with something so horrific was a power boost.

It reminded Piper of how they doused Gatorade on the football players in high school, and she had to cover her mouth to not only keep her jaw from falling to the floor but to also stifle her laughter.

She backed away from the door, not giving a damn that she hadn't pulled the door shut, and hurried to her apartment. Let another poor bastard suffer the hilarious, unimaginable, soul-shaking misfortunate she just had.

CHAPTER 7

"Was Dagger any trouble?"

"Not at all. I even took him for a walk after work each day, and we had some pretty good conversations. He's quite wise."

"He is. I get all my stock tips from him."

"You're silly. How was your trip?" she asked.

"It was much needed. I hadn't seen my grandparents in a while, and it felt good. They live on a 25-acre farm in Alabama, so it was also a mental vacation of sorts."

Piper wondered if he went with anyone. Well, not just anyone. Legs, to be exact, but she didn't want to ask.

"Twenty-five acres? That's a lot."

"It is, but someone takes care of the farm for them."

Desmond was standing right inside the door. He noticed her suitcase.

"Your vacation starts tomorrow, I remember. Where are you going?"

"I wouldn't call it a vacation."

"What would you call it?"

"A funeral."

"Damn. I'm sorry. Why didn't you tell me? All you said was that you had to go out of town Thursday, and I just assumed you meant for vacation."

Piper smiled because he looked so apologetic.

"It's totally fine, Desmond. I don't take offense. I knew what you might have assumed and didn't correct you. The idea of a vacation instead was nice, plus I wasn't interested in talking about it."

"Is there anything I can do for you?"

She tilted her head.

Why was he so nice? What was his aim?

"No. You've already done enough, and I appreciate it. It's for my Aunt Delores. She was like a mom to me. Losing her hurts more than I ever imagined, but I'm okay."

"How long will you be gone?"

"Only until Saturday."

He gave her another look of sympathy.

"If you change your mind, you'll let me know, right?"

Piper nodded.

"Let's go, Dagger. Piper needs her place back."

He waved goodbye, and Piper slowly closed the door. She didn't want him to go. His presence and sense of humor were comforting.

"Get over it, girl. You have enough problems," she said aloud.

Leaning against the door, she slid down to the floor. Aunt Delores was gone, finding a new job had been a failure, and her love life was . . . tricky. What a load of shit she was in.

"My condolences to you and your family," the older woman with the big hat said.

Her name was Helen, or maybe it was Mary. All the women in the big church hats were a blur. They would come by, lay a hand on her shoulder, and offer words of encouragement or comfort to her and Russell.

The woman moved along, placing a casserole on the table. It fit perfectly with the other three that were sitting there. The table also included pies, cookies, baked loaves of bread, and something odd-shaped with foil wrapped around it.

Russell and his roommates would be set for quite some time in the food department. Piper didn't want any of it, although Russell would likely offer, it somehow didn't feel right.

The funeral had been pleasant. Guests took turns speaking kind words and reliving fun memories. Piper remained strong and didn't cry, although after seeing her aunt in the casket, she had to keep wiping her eyes to halt the outpouring of tears.

Aunt Delores was her dad's sister, which meant Chloe and Talia (cousins she felt closer to) had no relation to Aunt Delores and weren't there. Russell was the only person she knew here, and showing weakness would be considered an invitation for strangers to attempt to console her.

Besides, she had a ten-hour car ride back to Atlanta alone. All the tears that needed freeing were welcome to do so at that point.

When the last person left Russell's place, Piper was thankful the whole thing was over. The threat of remembering her aunt in a casket and all the melancholy surrounding this day was starting to get burned into her memory. She wanted to remember Aunt Delores as a strong woman with blunt advice and a bubbly personality.

"Hey, Russell. I'm not going to stay much longer. I need to get on the road. Do you need me to do anything for you before I leave?"

Russell looked around, his eyes landing on the crowded food table.

"You want some food?"

"No. You guys have at it. Thank you for letting me stay."

"It was no problem."

He looked down briefly and then shook his head. He and Piper weren't close. He was five years older than her and already a young adult concerned with living his life when she moved in.

Being with him these few days was fun, though. It made them both realize that developing a relationship would be a good idea.

"What's wrong?"

He exhaled.

"Mom is gone, and that kind of feels like it cuts ties between us. I was hoping we could keep in touch more."

"I'd like that. I'm also sure it would make Aunt Delores happy. I miss her already."

"I do too. If she were here, she'd say stop that sulking and go out and enjoy life."

"You should. I need to leave, though, but I'd like a rain check."

"I guess that means I'll be coming to Atlanta soon."

He put his arm around her, and some of the tears reserved for the car ride home arrived early.

"How was the funeral?" Lish asked.

It was Sunday afternoon. Piper had just gotten back from Miami at three that morning.

"You know funerals? Ever so lively."

"I told you I would have gone down with you."

"I know. It was a peaceful drive. I thought it would be horrible at first, but it turns out it was calming."

"Want to hang out after you get off work on Friday? I'm going to be off work that night. My period will be visiting."

"Sure, you can also help me look for new apartments. I need to find something more affordable since I—"

Her phone beeped, and she looked at the caller ID. Her heart skipped a beat. It couldn't be.

"Piper, are you there? What were you going to say?"

"Lish, let me call you back," Piper said, not even waiting for a response before ending the call.

"Hello."

"Hi. May I speak with Piper Fosters?"

"This is she."

"Ms. Fosters, this is Yolanda Newbury calling you from Juniper Creek Medical. If you are still available, we would like to offer you the Executive Administrative position."

Piper's mouth fell open, and it took her a second to realize she hadn't responded.

"Yes. I'm still interested."

"That's wonderful. We would need you to start in two weeks on the 23rd. Would that provide you with enough notice for your current employer?"

Piper didn't give a shit if it wasn't enough notice. Mrs. Friedman was getting her sayonara regardless.

"That's enough time."

Yolanda supplied more details concerning what the company needed her to bring on the first day. The woman also sent a detailed email that included an entire layout of the job responsibilities, salary, and new employee frequently asked questions.

As soon as the call was over, Piper thanked God and did a happy dance while smiling so hard her cheeks burned. The pay for this job would take care of all her financial troubles. No need to move, strip, or feel obligated to accept handouts. Best of all, cable and Wi-Fi were about to make their way back into her life.

Piper began dancing again.

"I did it, Aunt Delores. I did it!" Piper said, overcome with excitement, happy tears, and exhilaration.

She needed to call Lish back, Scott, and anyone else who would listen. Grabbing her phone, Piper paused when she heard a knock at the door.

"Who is it?"

"Desmond."

Piper yanked open the door and surprised Desmond and herself by jumping into his arms. He held two items in his hand and quickly shifted to avoid them from being squished.

"Someone's happy. Did you win the lottery?"

"Pretty much," she replied, pulling him inside. "I just landed the job of my dreams."

"That's what I'm talking about!" he cheered, giving her a high five. "What will you be doing?"

"I," she said, straightening her clothes and pulling on her most dignified face, "will be an Account Executive at Juniper Creek Medical."

Desmond put the packages down on the kitchen counter.

"Wow, congratulations, Piper. I knew you could do it."

They stared at one another as the smiles and laughs slowly faded into something more heated and intense. Stepping back, Piper cleared her throat.

"So, what's up? Did you forget something for Dagger?"

"No. I wanted to drop off dinner. I know losing someone you love is hard, and the last thing anyone wants to do is cook. I would have done it yesterday, but you were just getting back from Miami, and I didn't want to disturb you."

"That's sweet," Piper said, looking at the square covered tray. "What is it?"

"Casserole."

Piper tried to give him her best smile. A casserole was the last thing she wanted but appearing ungrateful would be cruel.

Desmond started laughing.

"I'm kidding. You should have seen your face. It's spaghetti cooked in a red wine sauce."

"Now that is more like it! But your joke was mean. The last thing I want to see is another casserole."

"I figured as much."

"Why does everyone always bring those anyway?" she asked.

"Beats me. I think it's because it keeps easy. Pop it into the freezer, already prepped, and then into the oven when you're ready."

"Makes sense."

She picked up the vanilla-padded envelope Desmond brought inside with him.

"What's this?"

"Oh, that's yours. It was outside your door. I guess one of the neighbors was given your mail by mistake."

"Mail mix-ups have definitely happened in this building before. For a whole month, I kept getting stuff for Mr. Leo in 2C, and he wasn't happy about it."

"I've met him. He's a mean one."

"I think he's lonely," she said, tearing open the envelope.

After tilting it, a beautiful, glossy black box fell out.

Piper smiled and picked it up, undoing the tape on the sides. It must have been a surprise from Scott. At the beginning of their relationships, spontaneous gifts and outings were part of the norm. Lately, things hadn't been going so smoothly. It was time they got back to the way their relationship used to be.

I'll have to call him and say thanks. Then we can have a sexy face time chat and . . .

Piper dropped the box and screamed, and Desmond ran over.

"What's wrong—" he cut off abruptly. "Oh shit! Is that what I think it is?" he said, taking a step back in disgust.

"Yup," Piper said through clenched teeth.

The long square black box contained one thing. It was an item so grotesque and childish that Piper was sure she knew who'd sent it. Laying before her inside the lovely package that merely seconds ago, she'd admired and loved, was a bloody pad.

Piper would have been disturbed, nauseous, mortified even, but all of that took a back seat to how enraged she was. Simone, or whatever the fuck her name was, had struck again. Piper glanced at the envelope, and the front was completely blank, which meant the bitch had hand-delivered it.

Piper was in such a great mood about Juniper and enjoying Desmond's company that she didn't even inspect the envelope before opening it.

On the inside of the box's lid was a card that read:

I think you two disposables should be together.

"Why would someone do that to you?" Desmond asked.

"Because she doesn't value her life."

Piper opened the cabinet underneath her kitchen counter and retrieved some disposable gloves. Then opening a drawer, picked up a long-handled spoon.

"And because she wants me to break up with my boyfriend."

"That's umm . . ."

"Crazy, I know."

"So, she's some random girl?"

"No," Piper said, snapping the gloves in place. "She is his obsessed nanny."

"Damn, are you serious?"

"Afraid so."

"Wait, you said she is. Does she still work for him?"

"She does. Until he finds a replacement." Piper was getting more pissed by the minute.

Desmond said nothing. It was apparent he'd made a conscious decision to keep his mouth closed and his opinions to himself. His expressions, on the other hand, made no such agreement.

"Don't worry, Des. I feel the same way, but it's a long story."

Piper's movements were swift and furious. She pulled the trash can over to the counter where the despicable contents lay. Using the spoon, she pushed the envelope, nasty box, and its equally filthy lid into the trashcan. Then she dropped the spoon in as well before pulling the trash bag out and tying it up.

"I'm going to kill her," Piper said.

Desmond took the bag from her hand.

"I'll take this out. Listen, let's go somewhere. Anywhere. I think you need a breather."

"I don't want to go out. I want to commit a crime. Murder, to be exact."

"I know you think you do, but the anger will wear off, and then you'll still be in jail. You are too beautiful, too talented, and too important to be in jail. I don't understand this whole mess but step back before you go diving in. Sometimes a better way of handling an issue is right in front of your face."

His comment only made her mind form one question. Was Desmond implying that she should get rid of Scott? If so, it was something she'd considered many times. That was until her guilt rode in, and she recalled that she cared about him and Ryan.

"I'm too important?" she asked, finding something less complex about his comment to focus on.

He gave her the sexiest, sweetest grin ever.

"Haven't you heard? You're the new Administrative Executive at Juniper Creek Medical."

It was hard not to smile at a comment like that. Some of the tension eased, and she pulled off the gloves and sat in a chair.

"Let's go celebrate your win for today, Piper, because it is a pretty big win."

"You know what? You're right. After I shower a few times to rinse the foulness of crazy bitch off me, I'll meet you at your place."

Desmond took her to the last place she expected him to, skating. Since it was early in the day, they mostly had the rink to themselves. Piper couldn't remember the last time she'd been skating.

Having an inattentive mom and being the unwanted house guest of various family members didn't leave much time for recreational activities. But she had always enjoyed the skating, and now thanks to Desmond, the day was a fun reminder.

They spent most of the outing talking about her aunt, her new job, and Desmond's visit with his grandparents. Expectedly, Desmond stayed away from conversations concerning relationships. Piper knew it was because he didn't want to restart her fury, and for that, she was grateful.

Nonetheless, the gesture was a relief and a bummer. Piper

wanted to know once and for all if Legs was his girlfriend. However, opening that can of worms meant she might have to divulge information as well, and that was not an appealing conversation.

After skating, Desmond took her to grab a bite to eat at a small but cute lounge.

"You already delivered dinner to me. There was no need to take me out."

"Piper, we are celebrating, remember? I'm not going to accept any of your excuses. This is happening, so sit back and enjoy. Besides, you can save that delicious food for tomorrow."

Piper sat back in her chair.

"Des, can I ask you a question?"

"Definitely."

"Why did you help me? With the money?"

A waitress came over to take their orders and drop off two glasses of wine. Once the woman left, Piper made a face.

"What's wrong?"

"I don't normally drink wine; it's usually so bitter."

"I'm not big on wine myself, but this one is sweet, and we need something classy for when I make my toast."

"You just think of everything, don't you?"

She was poking fun at him, but the way he took charge while making her feel at ease was something that hadn't slipped her notice. Desmond knew how to charm a woman, and even if she shouldn't, Piper was relishing the moment.

"I try." He took a sip of his wine. His big hands, making the glass appear so small and fragile.

"What's your drink of choice?" he asked.

"Daiquiris."

He nodded slowly.

"Yeah, I can see that."

"How so?"

"A girly, fun drink. It fits you perfectly."

"Flattery will get you everywhere, but I haven't forgotten my original question. Why did you help me?"

"I have no idea what you're talking about. You helped me. I needed someone to watch Dagger."

She regarded him and his entire cool, confident vibe. This was wrong. Being out with him, wanting him, it was all so dangerous. He presented her with a high level of temptation, and she wanted in.

Locking eyes with him, Piper picked up her glass to sample the wine. True to his word, the wine was sweet. It was a white wine, fruity, crisp, and memorable. She closed her eyes and moaned.

"I like this."

"I thought you would."

When she opened her eyes, he was watching her, a fierce and prolonged gaze that Piper felt right between her legs. She instinctively tightened them. This heated silence had to stop.

"Do you normally travel a lot?" she asked, grasping at any subject that would halt the nasty scenes playing out in her mind.

"Not that much. I always said I should travel more, but I guess I haven't gotten around to it. My siblings and I plan on vacationing somewhere together one day soon, but we haven't sorted out the details."

"I'm so jealous. I wish I had siblings to do things like that with. Right now, we would be in Vegas, or Bali or even Japan living it up."

"Those are all places you want to go, I assume?"

"They are. Seems like there would be a lot of fun stuff to do. If you could do anything right now, what would it be?"

He was enjoying another sip of his wine when she asked

the question. Placing it back on the table, he asked, "Do you really want to know?"

"I do."

"Tasting you."

Piper licked her lips, and the words, those damn words that betrayed her fell out.

"All you had to do was ask."

He lifted a brow, and less than 15 minutes later, they were back at her place, having left a trail of clothes from the front door to her bedroom. Needless to say, they agreed to cancel dinner, opting instead to head straight to dessert.

And now, here they were. Desmond was towering over her as she lay on the bed, fully nude. Piper watched him intently. He was removing his last bit of clothing, and his body demanded her attention—long, lean muscles covered every inch of his almond-colored skin.

He motioned for her to come closer and then lifted her off the bed. She wrapped her legs around his waist and closed her eyes. The touch of his hands caressing her back caused her nipples to tighten and her most intimate area to pulsate.

"Piper?"

"Yes," she responded, staring into his eyes. She expected him to tell her how much he wanted her or how beautiful she was, but his next words caught her completely off guard.

"Dancers are flexible, right?"

"Huh?" was the only word she managed to say before Desmond raised her higher so that she was now sitting on his shoulders.

His mouth was inches away from her pussy, and her mind was still trying to decipher what had just happened.

He placed his hands on her ass, securing her position, and she felt the warmth of his breath right before his tongue began to tease, taste, and suck her pussy.

Piper momentarily lost the ability to speak, a guy had never eaten her out while standing, and it increased the thrill, while the talent of his mouth increased her wetness.

She could actually feel her juices flowing down her thighs. Wrapping her legs tighter around his neck and placing both hands on his head, she pressed harder against his face, and Desmond moaned his appreciation.

Already her orgasm was close, but when he took a few steps back and leaned against the wall, Piper delayed the release by placing her hands flat against the wall, rolling her hips, and sliding her pussy side to side and up and down.

She didn't want this to end. It felt too good, but Desmond had other plans. Using his tongue, he placed all the attention on her swollen clitoris, and the orgasm she'd been able to stall forced its way out, and she screamed his name as he continued to devour her.

When her breathing calmed, and her grip on his shoulders loosened, he tossed her back onto the bed.

"Shit, that was amazing," she said, still catching her breath.

He wiped his mouth and licked his lips, giving her a seductive grin. She sat up and pulled him down so that their lips met. She was hungry for him, and he mirrored the same need for her. Tasting herself and the faint traces of wine on his tongue, she pulled him closer, and the kiss deepened.

Running his fingers through her hair, Piper groaned into his mouth and arched her back, her fingers finding their way down his chest and stomach to grab his swollen member.

Pushing him back into a standing position, Piper eased down to the floor, taking his dick into her mouth. He mumbled a curse and tightened his grip on her hair. At first, her pace was deliberate, sliding his dick in and out of her mouth in a teasing manner, enjoying the hardness and salty taste of precum on her tongue.

Then Piper moved faster, adding her hand into the mix so that she was jacking him off and sucking his dick at the same time. The act was a massive turn-on. Getting a guy off had never felt this hot.

"Get up," he said, his voice husky and demanding.

Piper complied, and he lifted her into the air before falling onto the bed with her in his arms. Immediately Piper tried to take control. She needed to feel him inside her and satisfy the sexual ache for him that had been present since she first laid eyes on him.

"Why are you rushing?"

Breathless and tingling all over, she looked up at him. "What?"

"Do you know how long I've wanted you? I'm going to savor this."

And savor he did. He kissed her everywhere—her collarbone, stomach, back, and even her ass. Piper didn't know what to do with herself. Never had a man made love to her body before. Sex was always like a fast-paced ride, with both participants reaching the finish line in an explosion of pleasure. There was no prolonged foreplay, trance-inducing kisses, or moments of getting lost in each other's eyes.

Making his way back up her stomach, he stopped to spend time on each breast. Taking one hard nipple into his mouth, sucking and lightly biting it, while he squeezed and played with the other between his fingers. When she finally felt she couldn't take anymore, he gradually pushed into her inch by inch, igniting her body as whimpers and cries of pleasure escaped her lips.

He moved with an ease and familiarity that she hadn't thought possible as their bodies melted perfectly into one another. This was their first time, but it seemed like they had been one forever.

Her mind was clear of all problems, all sadness or pain

because she was lost in a private world that Desmond had created just for the two of them. They both came in a burst of fulfillment, so powerful and earth-shattering, it momentarily blurred Piper's vision.

Close to an hour later, Desmond got up and started getting dressed. Piper was done for. The euphoric cloud she was floating on was too comfortable to vacate. She watched him cover up that glorious body.

"No, stay naked," she said in protest.

He chuckled, pulling on a shoe.

"Then everyone would want some."

Piper sighed and said in a defeated tone, "Good point, go ahead and get dressed."

He straightened, approached the bed, and extended his hand.

"Walk me out?"

"You know where the door is."

"I do, but you have to lock up, don't you?"

"Dammit! I don't want to leave my cloud of pure bliss."

"I'll restore it whenever you want, I promise."

She rolled her eyes and got up. After opening the door, he turned to say goodnight.

"I enjoyed spending time with you today," he said.

"So did I."

He leaned down, kissed her on the forehead, and at that moment, everything was perfect.

CHAPTER 8

"**I** feel like such a slut, Lish."

"Piper, you are not a slut. And if you are, so what? Men are sluts too."

"Yes, but the plan isn't to join them. My slut behaviors begin and end in my mind. In there, I have slept with countless celebrities, all the men at the fire station on 5th, and that weird guy at the farmers market downtown."

"Oh, I know that guy. He is oddly cute, isn't he?"

"He is. But that's beside the point. Only in my head do I do these things. In reality, it makes me no better than Scott."

Piper collapsed onto the couch, picked up a red pillow in the shape of lips, and stared at it. It was purchased on a whim one night when she went out partying with Lish and two other girls from the club.

Piper saw the pillow on a souvenir rack in a convenience store. She was pretty drunk but swore the lips were talking to her, complimenting her on her dress and saying how great they would fit with her furniture. It could have been the alcohol talking, but the lips made some excellent points, and Piper purchased them immediately.

These days, the pillow no longer talked to her, but they were great for cuddling at stressful times.

"No, you are not like Scott. Scott is a piece of shit."

"Maybe so, but I still love him, and as outlandish as the whole nanny story is, if he is telling the truth and Simone is simply some obsessed girl, then that makes him the victim and me the cheater."

"And what does that make Desmond?"

"The other guy that I want but can't have. I don't love him, but I really like him, Lish."

She squeezed the pillow lips tighter. "But what difference does it make? He has a girlfriend, which proves my point. I'm still a low-life cheater!"

"Are you talking about Legs? So what? Maybe he will dump her."

"Lish! I don't want a man that I got by helping him cheat. Nor do I want to be some home wrecker."

"Whether you want to be a home wrecker or not, it looks like you are. He's about to dump Legs tonight, because you opened yours last night."

Lish laughed at her own joke, and Piper threw the pillow at her. It hit her on the top of the head before landing on the floor.

"I'm serious," Piper said.

"So am I! Desmond got him some Piper Pussy and Legs is as good as gone." She leaned towards Piper. "Was it as good as I think it was?"

"It was fucking better," Piper groaned. "I have never in all my days had a guy treat my body that way."

"So there will be a round two?"

"Lish the next thing I throw over there won't be soft."

"Ooh, will it be hard like Desmond's—"

Piper scooped a piece of ice out of her cup and threw it at her friend. This time it bounced off Lish's shoulder.

"Alright. Alright. I'll move on. Have you talked to Scott about that little stunt Simone pulled?"

"I did, and get this, he says Simone hasn't been back from her little emergency."

"What about Ryan?"

"He has had to stay with the grandparents until Scott can get someone new hired."

"Well, that's good news, isn't it? It means she's out of the picture?"

"I wouldn't say that because if I can't find her, I can't kill her."

"I'm with you there. After what she pulled, a nice, long stay in intensive care is well deserved."

Suddenly Lish jumped up and ran over to Piper, pulling her onto her feet.

"That reminds me. You got the job!"

Piper and Lish screamed in excitement and jumped around just like they'd done three times before whenever hospitals or anything medical was mentioned in their conversation.

"Lay the details out to me again. You start in two weeks?"

"No. I start in one week and three days, to be exact."

"This is so exciting. Have you told Mrs. Friedman?"

"I'm giving her my official notice Friday. That next week is my last week."

"What about Scott?"

"He is due in town next week also, so I plan to tell him in person. I know he's going to be happy for me."

"I'll bet he will. That way, he can forget his wallet all the time," she said sarcastically.

"Lish, it was an accident, and it's not like he hasn't helped me before."

"I know. I'm still mad at him about Simone, that's all. I'll be good, I swear. No more bad talk about Scott. I wouldn't want you to get mad and put me in the hospital."

They locked eyes and smiled.

"Did you say hospital?" Piper asked right before they held hands for the fourth time that day and screamed with joy.

Piper only needed to send two more emails concerning inventory for the clinic, and her day would be complete. She was in a good mood. Next week would be her final five days working there, Scott would be in town, and very soon, shopping and spontaneous fun would be back on her schedule.

There was still that one issue concerning Desmond, what the hell would she do about him? Thinking about it too long made her head hurt. Scott's disloyalty was under the spotlight all this time, and here it was, she was just as guilty.

The inner battle between doing what was right versus what was wrong tugged at Piper continuously. Should she come clean with Scott and cut Desmond off cold turkey? Or skip telling Scott and fuck Desmond's brains out every chance she got?

Neither scenario afforded true happiness. Her attraction to Desmond had grown and, the sex was the best Piper had ever experienced. But that didn't mean Desmond was good for her.

He'd cheated on his girlfriend, and that didn't make him a catch; that made him more chaos. What if his girlfriend found out? Then a new woman might be harassing her. Hell no. That was the last thing she needed. Desmond reached out to her a few times, but she kept the conversations short.

He told her he needed to speak to her and come clean

about something, and she pretended to be too busy. What would his confessions do at this point? They'd already slept together.

Why do I always choose the cheaters?

The thought prompted her to consider something else. Was all this drama with Simone merely Karma for not trusting and supporting Scott while she emotionally and eventually physically cheated on him with Desmond?

No. Now was not the time for this. It was a good day and the start to a great weekend. The familiar ache in her head was starting up again, which implied she was overthinking.

Her desk phone rang.

"Yes, Mrs. Friedman?"

"Piper, dear, can you come to my office, please?"

"Of course, I'll be right there."

She already knew what this was concerning. Mrs. Friedman wasn't in her office earlier, so Piper had left her letter of resignation on the desk. Apparently, Mrs. Friedman had now seen it and wanted to discuss it.

When she arrived at her boss's office door, it was open.

"Please, please come, sit down," Mrs. Friedman said, motioning Piper to the seat in front of her desk.

Once Piper sat, the woman steepled her fingers and gave Piper a long stare.

"You're leaving us, huh?"

"Afraid so," Piper said, forcing an adequate dose of sorrow into her tone.

"May I ask where you are going?"

"I was offered a position at a hospital."

Mrs. Friedman nodded.

"Is there any way I can get you to reconsider?"

"No, I don't think so."

"It's not the pay, is it? I pay you pretty good here, don't I?

The months of struggling to make ends meet flashed

through her mind. Why did companies always think their wages were so competitive when most employees could barely survive on them?

Piper answered her boss honestly.

"Unfortunately, no. The pay here doesn't fully cover my financial obligations."

"So it is the money. I paid you as much as I could."

"I'm sure you did, and I appreciate the opportunity."

Mrs. Friedman still didn't seem satisfied with losing her, and Piper wasn't surprised. She was a great employee that did too much work for too little pay.

"If I give you another quarter raise, will that fix it?"

"No, that's not—"

"Fifty cents!"

Where were all these supportive raises when Piper needed them? Mrs. Friedman wanted to play hardball, but she was about to play it alone. Leaving the company was not up for negotiation. Therefore, Piper decided to put the older woman out of her misery.

"It's not just the money, Mrs. Friedman. The distance works better for where I live, and I've always wanted to work in a hospital."

Her boss's lips formed into a firm line, and she exhaled.

"Well then. I guess we've lost you. If you change your mind, you can always return. Filling your shoes won't be easy."

Piper stood. Mrs. Friedman's predicament was her own, much like the love triangle Piper had gotten herself into. It wasn't very likely, but perhaps the clinic would pay their next hire a lot better.

"Thank you, Mrs. Friedman. I have to get back to work."

Exiting the office, she returned to her desk to finish the last tasks for the day. A quick cell phone check revealed an 'I love you, and I can't wait to see you next week' message from Scott.

Piper replied with similar sentiments and bit her lip. This situation was shitty.

After getting home, Piper pulled out the ingredients for tacos. The last few weeks Jake had come over, he was sad that he couldn't watch his favorite shows. Piper was hoping that one of his favorite meals would make him happier tonight.

Right on time, Daya arrived with Jake looking around, hoping desperately that something had changed.

"Sorry, Buddy," Piper said, pulling him in for a hug. "Still no cable."

Jake looked down at his shoes.

"I guess it's more toy robots and card games then. I'll go set up my things."

"Hold on just a minute. I have two sets of good news for you."

His face instantly changed as his eyes lit up, and an overexcited smile replaced the frown.

"What is it?"

"First thing. I got a new job, so I will be getting the cable back soon."

"Soon as in next week?" he asked, practically jumping up and down.

"No, not that soon. I have to get my first check and then get some things back in order."

"Why does it have to take so long?"

Her plan to give him good news was certainly backfiring. Piper looked at Daya, and the woman shrugged.

"Don't look at me. He always has tons of questions."

Piper decided to move on to door number two.

"Never mind all that. Tonight, I am cooking you one of your favorite meals."

"Chicken nuggets?"

"No, the other one."

"Grilled cheese?"

Piper looked to the ceiling.

"The other one."

"Hot dogs and tater tots?"

"I give up. I made you tacos, Jake. I thought you liked tacos."

"Sometimes I do, other times, I don't."

Piper threw her hands in the air.

"Go ahead and set up your toys, sweetie. I need to talk to Piper before I go," Daya said.

"That kid is a handful," Piper said.

"Tell me about it," Daya agreed. "But speaking of good news. I have some for you."

She pulled out her wallet and withdrew a $100 bill.

"I can start paying you back the money you loaned me."

Piper shook her head.

"Daya, you don't have to."

"No, I want to. Actually, I need to. It's the right thing to do."

"Are you sure? I was never holding you to it. And if you hadn't heard, I got a new job, so things are looking up for me."

"You deserve it, but you also deserve your money back."

She pulled Piper's hand, placed the money inside, and closed it.

"I don't know what we would have done without you. You're the reason I got to stay with my son while he healed."

Piper pulled her in for a hug, and Daya hugged her back before sniffling.

"I'm getting all teary-eyed. I need to get to work."

She said goodbye to Jake and was out the door.

Piper viewed the rest of the weekend as foreshadowing the shifts and changes her life was about to take. Taco night on Friday with Jake was a hit, and he even requested it again when he returned the following week.

Lish came over, on Saturday and they went to a small house party of a common acquaintance.

Sunday, Piper used her phone to do some online shopping for new clothes and shoes. The items never made it out of the virtual cart, but knowing that they were ready and waiting when she did have the money gave her the familiar shopping high she had grown used to.

The less enjoyable part of her weekend was speaking to Desmond. More so, breaking the news to him that the other night was a mistake that would not repeat itself. However, after catching a glimpse of him in the parking lot talking to Legs, Piper once again postponed the conversation.

I'll talk to him on Monday or Tuesday, she thought to herself.

But with the way life unfolds, an opportunity never came. Her last week at the clinic was hectic because Mrs. Friedman tried to get every last bit of her money's worth out of Piper.

Every day, Piper cleaned out the newly vacated animal cages, restocked inventory, ran errands, and helped Mrs. Friedman re-organize parts of the office.

Piper dragged herself home at the end of each workday, fatigued and achy. On Thursday, when Jake came over, she made him the tacos she'd promised last week and then fell asleep on the couch until Daya returned from work to pick him up.

On her last day, things were still pretty rushed, but everything Mrs. Friedman tossed at her got handled, and at the end of the day, Piper happily said goodbye . . . forever.

Scott arrived at her place a few hours after she got there. The joy of telling him about her new job would have to wait until after dinner. Telling him over the phone didn't seem exciting enough, and now that he was here, letting him get settled in first made more sense.

She'd planned a special dinner for them to celebrate. A restaurant nearby made delicious grilled steaks. Piper saved a little grocery money to pick up two of them and planned to make the sides at home.

"Hi, sexy. I missed you."

Scott dropped his bags next to the kitchen island and wrapped his arms around her waist, pulling her close.

"I missed you too."

Immediately he started kissing her and undoing her shirt. Piper tried to stay in the moment, but it wasn't easy. Desmond kept popping up in her head. It was his lips on her mouth, his hands on her body, and his moans in her ear, not Scott's.

Suddenly she pulled away.

"I'm sorry. I've had a long week, and I'm on my period."

It was the most convenient lie her mind could locate.

"Damn, you didn't say anything on the phone about it. You know the first thing I always want is to be close to you when I get back."

"I know, so do I, but . . ." she shrugged, letting the gesture complete her sentence.

"He pulled her in close again.

"Maybe we can't have sex, but there are other things you could do for me."

Piper took the hint and agreed simply to leave the topic.

"Sure, after dinner. I have some good news to share with you."

"Really? What?"

"I'm not telling right now. How's Ryan?"

"He's good. Still with his grandparents."

"And Simone?"

"Well, Simone hasn't returned. She called and said her emergency was taking longer than expected. It's worked out, though, because Ryan's grandparents agreed to keep him when I'm not here until I could get someone new in."

"That's not too much for them? I know you initially thought they couldn't handle him full time."

"I ended up telling them what was going on, and they volunteered. They promised me it would be no trouble, and I promised them that getting the replacement won't take much longer."

Piper should be thrilled with the news but Simone not returning also meant Piper could never get her hands on the woman. Oh well, it was likely for the best. Spending time in jail wouldn't pair easily with her new positive, successful life plans. Also, hopefully, now that Scott had let her go, there would be no more harassment.

Scott rubbed his chin apprehensively.

"What's wrong?"

"Um, I hate to ask you this, but do you have a little money I can borrow? Things are still a little tight for me."

Piper thought of the $100 Daya had given her. It was in her wallet. She hadn't needed it because keeping a stringent budget proved to make an impactful difference.

"Yeah. I do, and don't worry about paying it back. It's part of my good news."

Retrieving the money, Piper handed it to him. She also spotted some mail that had come for him on her kitchen counter and gave that to him as well.

He held up the envelope.

"Thanks for this and the money. You have no idea how much you've helped me. This news you plan to share must be amazing?"

"Oh, it is."

Something Lish said a while back sprang to mind.

"Hey, I was wondering. Not that I mind helping, but aren't you due some type of worker's compensation because of the accident?"

Scott seemed caught off guard by her question but then collected himself.

"You know how jobs can be. They are dragging their feet."

He kissed her again—this time letting his lips trail down her neck and shoulder before stopping.

"What would I do without you?"

Piper smiled.

"I'm going to go get cleaned up before this wonderful dinner you've set for us," he said.

Piper closed her eyes as his hand gently caressed her face. He pulled away and went into the bathroom. Her nerves were a little jumpy. The secret she was harboring was eating away at her.

But everything is going to be okay. Tell him about it on Sunday before he leaves.

Telling him before he went back out of town was the cowardly way out, but it was the course she'd chosen. It gave her a bit of peace to know she wouldn't have to keep this secret much longer.

However, things got sidetracked because, to her horror, Desmond showed up.

"Uh, Hi, Desmond," she said after swinging the door open."

"I need to talk to you. As I have been trying to do all week but, you're good at dodging."

She gave a nervous smile.

"Busy week. Now isn't a good time, though."

"When would be a better time?"

At that very moment, Scott walked out of her bedroom.

Not wanting anything to look suspicious and remembering the dispute that happened the last time Scott saw Desmond at her door, Piper introduced the men to one other.

"Desmond, this is my boyfriend, Scott. Scott, this is my neighbor, Desmond."

Both men gave curt nods in the direction of the other. There was unspoken tension in the air, and Piper found herself very uncomfortable.

"Sorry to bother you, Piper. I'll catch you another time," Desmond said and walked away.

He didn't seem mad, but happy wasn't a suitable description either. Piper closed the door and faced Scott.

"What did he want?" His voice was cold and direct.

"I'm not sure. Maybe to ask a question about the building or something."

"Didn't look like it. You have something you want to tell me?"

"No."

Her eyes darted from one side of the room to the other.

Dammit, averting the eyes! Come on, Piper, that is a dead giveaway.

"Desmond is just a friend."

"Oh, he's a friend now?"

"You don't have to say it that way."

"I didn't say it any type of way, but please enlighten me. What makes the two of you friends?"

Piper searched her mind for something that sounded innocent enough.

"He paid me to watch his dog, which in turn provided me with the rest of the money to attend my aunt's funeral."

Scott narrowed his eyes.

"I thought you got the money up by returning to the Golden Bar?"

"I got some of the money that way but keeping the dog for him helped me get the rest."

"And you didn't think to tell me that?"

"No, I didn't. It was no big deal."

Scott began pacing the floor. His irritation was evident and unmerited.

"It's no big deal when it's you and some guy, but you broke it off with me when it was about Simone."

"That's not even the same. You kissed Simone, and that lunatic has been harassing me."

"I told you I didn't kiss her. She kissed me!"

"Alright. I got my facts mixed up. The point is, we have to trust each other, right?"

This night was going horribly. Building a case for herself on the grounds of trust, only to tear it down Sunday, was the dumbest idea she'd had in a while. The conversation kept moving forward, and she didn't know how to stop it. Admitting that something had happened with Desmond made her seem like she was always a lying cheater when that was not the case.

Scott took a step closer to her, and it felt strange. Reflexively Piper almost took a step back but instead wrapped her arms around herself and stood her ground.

"We don't have to trust each other," he said. "You need to trust me. I haven't done anything wrong. You, on the other hand . . . who knows? I don't want you talking to him anymore."

"What do you mean, who knows?"

Defending herself came naturally, but Piper needed to stop while she was ahead. At this rate, not telling him she'd cheated sounded like a better plan.

"You know what I mean. I don't like how he looks at you, and I damn sure don't like that he gave you money."

"It was for watching his dog, Scott."

"Why in the hell would you need money from him when you had a job to go to?

Now Piper found herself needing to keep her composure.

"Because maybe I didn't want to go to that job. Ever think of that?"

"No, I guess I didn't. A job is a job."

She stared at him bewildered.

"Do you have any idea how difficult it was for me to go back to stripping even for that one night? I promised my aunt and myself that I would not return once I quit, but as soon as things got tough, that is exactly what happened."

"Oh, please give it a rest. It should mean nothing for you to show your body off to strangers. They've already seen it all. Stop making excuses about promises you made to yourself and your aunt, who is no longer here to tell you what she thinks and stay the fuck away from that guy."

Piper picked up a glass and threw it at him. It just missed his head and crashed against the wall.

"What the fuck is wrong with you?"

She saw his hands ball into a fist, and then he released it.

"You need to calm down, Piper."

"And you need to get out before you regret being here!"

She added actions to her threat by picking up his workbag and shoes and shoving them into his arms.

"I want you out of here."

He took his things, unable to do much else with her sudden burst of anger playing out. Yanking open the door, Piper gave him another push, this one landing him outside the door.

"Piper, I'm sorry, let's talk about—"

She cut him off by slamming the door in his face.

He kicked the door, and she jumped.

"Are you serious?" Scott yelled from outside.

Ignoring him, Piper picked up her cell phone and inserted her earpiece. While loading a song to play, she heard him yelling and swearing outside the door. The song started up, and with the volume up to the highest notch, Scott's voice disappeared, and the music pulled her into a place that knew no pain, no drama, and gratefully, no Scott.

CHAPTER 9

"Paging Dr. Wagner. Paging Dr. Wagner," the voice said over the intercom.

Piper looked up from her paperwork and smiled. This all felt like a dream. Was she really here? So far, the journey of life had taken her from being an unwanted child to a stripper, then a college grad, and now an Account Executive for a well-known hospital.

It was all still so hard to believe. Aunt Delores would be so proud, and actually so would Russell.

Piper snapped a quick selfie and sent it to Russell with a brief message that read, "Hi! Guess who's an Account Executive?"

With the sharing mood still pulsating through her, Piper also sent the image to her cousins Chloe and Talia.

Lish had already received close to 10 selfies that morning as Piper tried to figure out which outfit made her appear most professional. Scott wasn't getting shit from her after how hurtful he'd been, and Desmond crossed her mind but sending him a pic would open up communication.

Avoiding 'the talk' with him for as long as possible was

her new plan. It wasn't very likely that it would last too long, but a girl could hope. Seeing him made her want to touch him, and touching him is how this whole mess started.

She already surmised he had a girlfriend, cheated on, said girlfriend, and wanted to come clean to Piper, but an explanation was unnecessary. As far as Piper was concerned, things were fine as is. They wouldn't hook up again, plain and simple.

There was a knock at Piper's office door.

"Hi, Piper. How is everything coming along?"

"Great!"

It was the operations manager and Piper's boss, Jada Wright. The woman was tall, with chestnut brown hair cut short and a face full of freckles. Piper guessed her age to be mid-thirties.

"Did you finish the new hire documents?"

"Yes, I did," Piper said, locating them underneath a folder."

"Wonderful. I'll take those. What do you have left?"

"Currently, I'm completing the short quiz on Chapter 1-5 of the employee handbook."

"Wow, you're fast." Jada checked her watch. "Don't forget lunch is at 12:30 in the break-room, and the company has already paid for it. It's our little welcome to the team gift for you and the two other staff members that started today."

"I'll be there," Piper said with a smile. "And thank you."

"No problem. If you need anything, my extension is already on your phone. You're going to do great."

Jada gave Piper a thumbs up and left the office, but her words of encouragement remained behind. Amid all the joy and excitement, admittedly was a sliver of apprehension.

Can I do this? Is my experience enough? Will the other employees like me?

Piper thought about it. Of course, everything would turn out fine. Having faith in her abilities was the key. At the veterinary clinic, she'd done an outstanding job. There was no reason the same couldn't happen here.

Her cell buzzed on her desk. It wasn't a number she recognized, so she hit the button sending it to voicemail. A few seconds later, it buzzed again with a different number.

Two unfamiliar numbers seconds apart was an odd occurrence. Glancing at the time on her computer, it indicated that lunch would start in thirty minutes. She'd call back on her break.

Picking up the pencil, Piper resumed taking the test. Her phone began to buzz again—another unknown number. Something was wrong. Sliding back away from the desk, she answered the call.

"Hello?"

"I'm looking for a good time. Where do you want to meet?"

"You have the wrong number," she said and hung up.

The phone vibrated again.

"Hello?"

"My dick is hard right now. You should come over and put it in your mouth, and I'll treat you like the worthless slut you are."

"Who the fuck is this?"

The guy grunted, and Piper could hear wet sounds coming from the other end.

Was he jacking off?!

"I like a woman with an attitude. Stop playing with me bitch and come get this money."

She pressed the end call button and covered her mouth.

What is going on? Who was that guy, and why was he calling me?

The phone vibrated to life yet again.

"Who is this?" she said into the receiver.

"The man that can't wait to get you into his bed tonight."

"Where did you get my number?"

"Who the hell cares. You'll do anything for twenty dollars, right?"

"Yeah, if that includes separating your balls from your body."

"You're a feisty one, Piper. I like it. Where do you want to meet?"

She ended the call again and swallowed. Her pulse was racing.

He knew her name. How did he know her name? The phone shook with yet another incoming call.

"How did you get this number?" she said immediately upon answering.

"The ad you posted in an online chat group. Did you mean it when you said anything goes?" The guy lowered his voice, "Like anything?"

He sounded young, and Piper fought hard to table her rage to collect more information.

"I was high when I wrote that. What did I say?"

"That you would do anything for $20, and the nastier, the better. How do I set something up?"

"You don't, asshole," she said, pressing her new favorite button.

The phone buzzed again, but this time the caller ID said unknown. Abrupt clarity flooded her brain.

Simone.

"You will pay for this," Piper threatened, answering the call.

"Aww, is someone having a bad day?" Simone asked as if speaking to a child.

Piper tightened her fist and bit her tongue to stop from screaming at the top of her lungs. She was seething, and the office seemed to be getting very warm. Even her palms were sweaty.

"What did you do?" Piper said with a jaw clenched so tight it was a wonder Simone could make out her words.

"I only put out a little referral for you, that's all. I figured a whore like you could show those guys a good time."

Piper's other line beeped. She didn't even waste a second checking it.

"If I ever get my fucking hands on you, you're dead."

"Promises. Promises," Simone mocked, brushing off the threat. "Listen, I don't want you to see Scott again, and if you do, I'll know."

"One day, you will slip up, and when you do, I am going to make you sorry."

Simone giggled. Fucking giggled as if this was a joke. Piper mentally noted the laugh. The woman wouldn't be laughing when Piper finished with her.

"Don't piss me off, Piper, or next time I'll provide an address to go with the phone number. That way, your eager customers can visit you. Have a good day. And oh yeah, don't worry if you have to get a new number, I'll be in touch. As long as you are messing with my Scott, I'll find you."

Piper sat quietly in her office for the next five minutes. She couldn't speak. Her thoughts were hazy, and her breathing was loud and ragged. Being this upset had to be unhealthy.

Her phone continued to vibrate on her desk until she could steady her hand enough to turn it off.

When the alarm on her computer chimed to remind her about lunch, she didn't get up from her desk. It wasn't as if she had an appetite, so instead of meeting her fellow team members and playing nice, Piper continued to sit and stare.

How in the hell could she locate Simone? Scott had to know where that piece of shit was, and it was in his best interest to tell her.

Get a hold of yourself, Piper. There are good things in your life; remember the good stuff. Don't let Simone ruin this day.

She decided to take a quick break and grab a bottle of water from the lunchroom, and catch the tail end of the lunch celebration. Piper mustered up the brave face that she believed she was incapable of conjuring and enjoyed a brief meet and greet with some of her coworkers.

The sour mood that had invaded her body earlier had lifted slightly. It was good to step away, and now it was imperative to get back to work.

Before leaving the office for the day, Piper forced herself to be productive and finish the quizzes related to the employee handbook.

She also turned her phone back on and saw numerous congratulations texts from her cousins and 35 unheard voicemails.

One thing was for sure, she and Scott were over. Not because she feared Simone, aka dead girl walking, but because Piper wanted nothing to do with him after the way he treated her the other night. Top it off with the psychotic nanny, and it was a done deal; Scott wasn't worth fighting for.

When Piper returned home, she checked her mail as usual.

"Fuck!"

One of the letters had Scott's name on it. This madness had to end. Piper wanted nothing more to do with him and no traces of the asshole in her life. As soon as she was inside, Piper called Scott, ready to give him an ear full.

While waiting for him to answer, her other line beeped. The constant calls pouring in had slowed, but calls were still coming in every half hour or so.

When the call to Scott went to voicemail, Piper cursed again. Everything was always on his terms. Even if he wasn't cheating, this arrangement had idiot written all over it, and every arrow pointed at her. There was no way to find him unless he wanted to be found.

She couldn't remember how to get to his place, had no other way to reach him, in case of . . . wait, there was a way to locate him, his job. What was the name of it again? Piper closed her eyes and visualized the name written on that book bag he always carried around.

Lancer Communications.

A quick Google search displayed the only Lancer Communications in Milwaukee. Piper dialed the number and waited.

"Lancer Communications, this is Jasmine. How may I help you?"

"Hi, I'm trying to reach one of your employees, Scott Bolden."

There was a long pause, and then the woman lowered her voice.

"Who is this?"

"My name is Piper. Isn't this Lancer Communications?"

"It is, but Scott Bolden doesn't work here. In fact, I don't think that bastard works anywhere, but if you see him, tell him I want my money back."

CHAPTER 10

"Now, who the fuck is Jasmine?!" Lish asked, shocked.

Her paintbrush paused in mid-air, dripping pink paint onto the floor.

Piper and Lish were at a Paint and Sip event downtown. Lish was trying to create a woman in a sexy dress on her canvas, and Piper was painting a car. Both images were laughable and proved that a lot of adults still painted on a child level.

"I don't know! Whoever she is, she's pissed at Scott. But the bigger question is, why did she say he doesn't work there?"

"I'm guessing cause he doesn't."

"So where the hell does he work then?" Piper questioned a little too loud.

A few heads turned in their direction, and Piper lifted a hand in apology.

Speaking quieter, she said, "Lish, this is bad. Has he been lying about everything, including his feelings for me?"

"I don't know, sweetie. This is deep and beyond anything

I'm familiar with. All the men I dated were pretty much assholes to my face. Scott is on another level, it seems. Have you called him again?"

"No, I don't want to call him. I told you we are in a fight. One that ends us for good."

"He's the only one that can answer any of your questions."

"He's also the only one who can tell me where Simone is."

"Oh yeah, her. That girl isn't tied up in your trunk yet?" Lish asked the question casually, part of her concentration back on painting.

"You know she won't show her face."

"Which means she's smarter than she seems. Have the perverted calls stopped?"

"For the most part. I only get around one per day."

"If I didn't hate her so much, I'd want to be her friend. The girl is ruthless," Lish said.

Piper nudged her.

"You love juicy gossip."

"I can't help it. You think now that you are done with Scott, she will leave you alone?"

That was a long shot, and Piper wouldn't hold her breath. However, what astonished her the most was that killing Simone was not her main focus for now. This new development that brought Jasmine to light was taking up a lot of her time.

"I think I'm going to call the woman back at Lancer Communications."

"I would. Why didn't you call her back immediately?"

"She was at work and sounded pissed. I got the impression that talking about Scott was not her favorite subject, and then when she hung up on me, it was confirmed. I plan on giving it a few days, while I figure out exactly what I need to ask."

Piper added more red to the bulky car she was painting and took another sip of wine.

"Do you think he was involved with her while with you?" Lish asked.

That was a question Piper had also pondered. She picked up her glass and gulped the rest of the wine.

"There are so many lies swimming around Scott. I am starting to lose track."

"That's fair," Lish said, putting down her brush. "Now on to the fun question. Does Des giving you the dick have anything to do with your recent disinterest in Scott?"

Piper thought about it.

"I don't know it could, but Des was a one-time thing."

"Lish blew out a breath and rolled her eyes.

"So you keep saying. Have you talked to him yet? I'll bet he won't agree.

"I went by his place and got no answer. I haven't even seen him around these past few days."

Lish shrugged and smiled.

"Maybe Simone kidnapped him?"

"I wouldn't doubt it."

"Does my painting look good?" Lish asked. "I keep feeling like the woman and the dress simply resemble a stick figure standing inside of a triangle."

Piper titled her head.

"Yup, sorry, friend, you've painted a line through a triangle."

"Shit, I can't hang this up at home. I thought I'd be proud of it. I guess I'll sit it on my dresser instead."

"Mine isn't much better. The wheels aren't even connected to the car; they just hoover around the vicinity."

"Very true. My two-year-old nephew could do better."

In response, Piper reached over and grabbed Lish's glass of wine and finished it for her.

"Hey!" Lish objected.

"Shouldn't have picked on me. What are we doing after this?"

"Want to go to another party? I know you're all important now; maybe you don't want to hang with us stripper girls."

"I always got time for a good party," Piper said with a wink.

The hangover Piper was experiencing was excruciating.

It was a lot of fun making it, but now that it was possibly ripping apart her brain, Piper was rethinking last night's actions. It was all Lish's fault.

Nope, that was a lie. Piper was in full-blown 'I got a new job' mixed with 'my heart is broken' party mode. She brought this all on herself.

Thank goodness it was Sunday; she would be useless for the rest of the day.

The shrill ringing of her phone made Piper squeeze her eyes shut and wince. Forgetting to turn that off was a big mistake. Blindly reaching for it, she lifted it and opened one eye. It was Scott.

"What?" she growled

"You're still mad, huh?"

"I'm not mad. I'm done."

"I didn't mean those things I said. You know that?"

Piper moved the phone around while squinting, attempting to find the speaker button. Letting too much light in burned her eyes, which in turn increased the pressure in her head. Ultimately, she found the button, hit it, and then dropped the phone. It landed on the bed next to her.

"I called you at your job."

There wasn't enough energy in her body to say it in a tone that portrayed how angry and hurt she was. Besides, those emotions were pointless anyway. She and Scott were over.

He was silent for the longest time before asking, "Why?"

"Because I couldn't reach you. I'm done waiting on you to do things on your schedule."

"That's no reason to call me at work. Are you trying to get me in trouble?"

Ignoring his question and her pounding head, Piper moved on to her next thought. Hangovers were not new for her, but a man with this many secrets was.

"But you don't work there, do you?"

"Of course, I do. You're acting weird."

"Jasmine doesn't seem to think I'm weird."

Scott didn't miss a beat with his reply, and if Piper weren't so weak, she might have had the energy to question her own sanity.

"Who is Jasmine?"

"Scott, please stop it. All the lies are catching up to you."

"Piper, I promise you, I don't know who that is. I don't work out of the main building."

"How convenient," Piper said as she wondered why the room was spinning even with her eyes closed. Never again would she have wine, vodka, and rum in the same night.

"Where can I forward this mail you received? To Simone? Or maybe Jasmine?"

"You are overreacting. How can I prove to you that I love you, and you've got this all wrong?"

"Deliver Simone to me so I can run her over."

Yeah, that was fair. Simone deserved to feel as bad as she did at this very moment.

"What has she done now?!" Scott asked.

"Does it really matter?"

"It does. I have no idea where Simone is, and I feel like this is all my fault."

Piper placed a hand over her closed eyes. It needed to be darker. A damp washcloth would be perfect right about now.

"That's cause it is your fault."

"Piper," he paused before saying anything more. Summoning up the audacity again, she guessed.

"Move away with me? Just you, me, and Ryan."

She instinctively sat up. Her head wasn't too keen on the abrupt shift in position and intensified its pounding. Piper lay back down and groaned.

"Just like that? Runaway from the issues. What about my life, Scott?"

"You can start a new one." Then with emphasis, he added, "We can start a new one. Don't you love me?"

That's when it hit her. The truth and the actual reason why things were over.

"I do, Scott but, it doesn't matter anymore. Love isn't enough."

"You can't mean that? Let's get away from here, and everything will go back to the way it was at first, you'll see."

Was he serious? He sounded serious. Therefore, he must be crazy. Running away wouldn't solve anything. Not to mention, Piper didn't want to move. Her life was going well, and she was happy. Scott didn't even know about her new job and all the wonderful things that were unfolding for her. The only issues came from him, and that situation was about to be rectified.

"No, Scott. But have fun wherever you move to. And oh yeah, Jasmine said you owe her some money."

She heard him giving yet another mouthful of excuses and pleadings before she hung up. The spinning in her head finally slowed. It was replaced with the sudden urge to vomit, and Piper did so all over the floor.

The following day at work, Piper's condition had improved. She spent most of the day on Sunday lying in bed and feeling crappy. Scott called again once or twice, and she let it go to voicemail. Then around 8 pm, her empty stomach began to protest. She made scrambled eggs with toast and fell asleep.

Now at work, her first assignment was to create the outpatient folders for the week. Initially, her nerves made a mountain out of a molehill, but the task was pretty simple.

First, select the necessary paperwork for the patient using the document selector screen. Next, print it out and then place it into a nice Juniper Creek Medical folder for pickup.

Piper followed the basic steps. This particular patient required 15 sheets. She carefully checked and rechecked everything necessary before sending it to the printer, and fifteen documents later, viola, Mr. Daniel Gaines, patient #456839, had all the information he would need.

"One down and another 102 to go."

The next patient file required 20 documents. Piper used the same process to ensure that no mistakes occurred and moved on to the third. By lunchtime, she had developed a good rhythm and printed a total of 25 packets. She was so caught up in the task that she would have worked through lunch. However, an alarm set last week reminded her.

Keeping busy had kept her mind on work, but now that the alarm had jarred her out of work mode, Piper realized she was starving. It wasn't like she'd eaten a lot yesterday.

After grabbing her wallet, she put the computer into sleep mode and exited her office.

She was locking the office door when about 20 feet away, a woman slipped, and items flew everywhere. Piper pocketed the door key and ran over to help.

"Shit," the woman said, quickly trying to collect pens that

were rolling in every direction. "That's what I get for rushing."

It seemed she was talking to herself, and Piper wasn't even sure the lady had noticed her approach. Bending down to grab a lipstick and a baby rattle, Piper passed it to the woman and continued to collect more things.

"Thanks," the woman said, shoving the items into her oversized bag without looking up. "When you're a wife and mom, your purse practically becomes a storage unit for the family."

Piper laughed.

"I usually don't even come down this hall, but I had a meeting, and this side is closer to the cafeteria, and . . . ugh, well, you get the rest."

"I do."

The lady wasn't kidding about the storage bag. Piper collected more toys, a pack of bandaids, two salt packs, a diaper, a small perfume bottle, and a notepad and pencil that read: nurses are the best.

"Here you go," Piper said.

The woman took the items from Piper's hands, but this time, she looked up, and Piper froze. Not just froze. The air left her lungs, her brain exploded, and her mouth went dry. She knew this woman, had seen this woman. But never in person, only in photos, photos that hung on the wall inside Scott's home.

"Thank you, for . . . are you alright?" the woman asked.

"I . . . I . . ." Piper's mind raced. "I think I forgot something major for work," she said slowly.

"Oh, I know how that can be. Life is always moving, and it's a struggle to keep up."

Piper laughed nervously. It was all she could do; this had to be a dream. No, this was a nightmare. The woman before her was Scott's wife, but Scott's wife was dead, wasn't she?

Well, obviously, this woman hadn't gotten the memo because she extended a hand and said, "Where are my manners? I'm Julia Bolden."

THE END OF BOOK 2

Are you ready for More?

Love is Salty (Book 3)

is available at Amazon.

If you enjoyed this book we would greatly appreciate a review on Amazon.

ABOUT THE AUTHOR

Nicki Grace is a wife, mother, and author addicted to writing, spas, laughing, and sex jokes, but not exactly in that order.

Luckily for you, someone gave her internet access, and now you get to experience all the EXCITING, SHOCKING, and HOT ideas that reside in her head. She loves to have fun and lives for a good story. And we're guessing so do you!

Read more about her and check out more books at nickigracenovels.com

f facebook.com/nickigracenovels
instagram.com/nickigracenovels

ALSO BY NICKI GRACE

Romance

The INEVITABLE ENCOUNTERS Series
Book 1: The Hero of my Love Scene
Book 2: The Love of my Past, Present
Book 3 : The Right to my Wrong

———⟨∽⟩———

The LOVE IS Series
Book 1: Love is Sweet
Book 2: Love is Sour
Book 3: Love is Salty

———⟨∽⟩———

Thrillers

The Splintered Doll
The Twisted Damsel

———⟨∽⟩———

Self-Help

The TIPSY COUNSELOR Series
The Tipsy Dating Counselor (Summary)

The Tipsy Dating Counselor (UNRATED)

The Tipsy Marriage Counselor

The Pregnancy Counselor

Printed in Great Britain
by Amazon